Jennings as Usual

By the Same Author

Jennings Goes to School
Jennings Follows a Clue
Jennings' Little Hut
Jennings and Darbishire
Jennings' Diary
According to Jennings
Our Friend Jennings
Thanks to Jennings
Take Jennings, for Instance
The Trouble With Jennings
Just Like Jennings
Leave it to Jennings
Jennings, of Course!
Especially Jennings!
Jennings in Particular
Trust Jennings!
The Jennings Report
Typically Jennings!

The Best of Jennings

PUBLISHED BY LUTTERWORTH PRESS

A Funny Thing Happened
Rex Milligan's Busy Term
Rex Milligan Raises the Roof
Rex Milligan Holds Forth
Rex Milligan Reporting

Anthologies

PUBLISHED BY FABER AND FABER
Stories for Boys
Stories for Boys: 2
In and Out of School

Jennings
as Usual

ANTHONY BUCKERIDGE

Collins
LONDON AND GLASGOW

First printed in this new edition 1973

For Geoffrey Anderson

ISBN 0 00 162134 3
© Anthony Buckeridge, 1959
PRINTED AND MADE IN GREAT BRITAIN BY
WM. COLLINS SONS AND CO. LTD.
LONDON AND GLASGOW

CHAPTER 1

MESSAGE RECEIVED

THERE is a world of difference between a sensible hobby and a passing craze. Out-of-school activities such as carpentry or model-making have always been looked upon as worthwhile occupations calling for some degree of skill and experience. Unfortunately, the same cannot be said for those wild enthusiasms which sweep through a school like a prairie fire—a sudden urge, for example, to make spectacles out of pipe cleaners, or to construct handy gadgets from milk bottle tops and empty toothpaste tubes.

As a rule, crazes of this kind do not last very long and are soon abandoned in favour of the next prevailing fashion. But from time to time an idea will emerge which seeks to achieve the dignity of a genuine hobby. . . . The Form 3 home-made, high-fidelity telephone system was a case in point.

For the first half of the Christmas term the succession of popular crazes at Linbury Court School followed a familiar pattern. Conkers—a purely seasonal pastime—gave place to a passion for making banjoes from circular biscuit tins and school rulers.

This was followed by the introduction of the home-made snorkel—a simple breathing apparatus consisting of a length of rubber tubing which enabled the wearer to remain submerged for short periods below the surface of the bath water. The device became extremely popular, for it was found that it could be used equally well for providing a current of air beneath the bedclothes when reading by torchlight after lights out.

As the mania spread, so more and more snorkels were improvised, until lockers, tuck-boxes and trouser pockets were crammed and bulging with tangled coils of flexible piping. The most successful type was the "dual-purpose, 21-inch luxury model," fashioned from a length of garden hose fitted with a funnel at each end. There was also an inferior brand made from the discarded inner tubes of bicycle tyres. This sort, however, was frowned upon by the enthusiast, as it tended to leak under water and to collapse completely beneath the weight of the bedclothes.

Then, shortly after half-term, came the "do-it-yourself" telephone. As usual it was Jennings who pioneered the latest craze. . . . And it was Jennings, as usual, who was largely to blame for the trouble which ensued.

The idea came to him just before school one Monday afternoon as he was rummaging through the muddled contents of his desk in search of a missing exercise book. It is unlikely that the bright idea was inspired in any way by his surroundings, for Form 3 classroom was a rather dreary room decorated in two shades of green distemper. The furniture consisted of seventeen ink-stained desks, a well-worn blackboard and a cupboard with a broken latch; while pinned to the picture rail were a number of unframed water colours painted by the members of the form during their Art lessons. It was seldom, however, that Jennings allowed his enthusiasm to be dampened by the somewhat cheerless surroundings of his classroom.

"You know what, Darbi," he remarked to his friend who was dredging the ink-well of a neighbouring desk. "If I was on the 'phone I could ring up and ask him if he's got it in the staff room."

His companion broke off in the act of harpooning a fragment of ink-sodden blotting-paper with a broken nib. "Who's got what in the staff room?" he demanded.

"My English book: it isn't anywhere in my desk. I think Mr. Carter must have collected them at the end of the lesson yesterday afternoon."

Darbishire creased his brow in a puzzled frown, striving to follow his friend's train of thought. It was not always easy to grasp straight away what Jennings was talking about, for his argument tended to leap from point to point like a cat on a hot tin roof. And, indeed, this air of restless activity was typical of his whole nature. An eager manner and a wide-awake look in his eyes gave a clear indication that the eleven-year-old John Christopher Timothy Jennings was always ready to play a leading part in the more lively aspects of boarding-school life.

Darbishire, on the other hand, was of a cautious and peace-loving disposition, though he did his best to trail along in the wake of his more impulsive colleague. What he lacked in ambition he made up in loyalty, for where Jennings led the way Darbishire always followed.

"I don't see what you're woffling about," Darbishire persisted, wiping his ink-splashed glasses with an off-white handkerchief. "If you think Mr. Carter's got your English book why don't you go and ask him?"

"That's what I shall have to do. I was only saying that I could save myself the trouble of stonking all the way along to the staff room if I could ring him up instead."

Darbishire snorted. "You must be crazy! If you think the Head's going to have our classroom put on the 'phone just to save you wearing your legs out, you must want your brains testing."

"I don't mean a *real* telephone.. I mean a home-made one," Jennings explained patiently. "I read an article in an Annual last holidays that told you all about it. It's ever so easy, really. All you need is a couple of cocoa tins joined together with a long piece of string."

"And then what?"

"Well, that's all really. You talk into one of the tins and somebody else listens with the other one."

Darbishire pursed his lips doubtfully. "That'd never work in a million years," he objected.

"It jolly well would: the article said so," Jennings maintained. "It's strictly scientific, you see. The sound waves go hopping along the string and make the bottom of the cocoa tin vibrate like machine-gun fire."

The look of doubt remained on Darbishire's face as he replaced his glasses and ran his gaze along the rows of empty desks around him. "I still say it can't be done," he said, with a shake of his head. "You're overlooking one big snag."

7

"And what's that?"

"We haven't got any cocoa tins."

Jennings thumped his desk in mild exasperation. "But you great addle-pated clodpoll, Darbi, they don't *have* to be cocoa tins! Any old tins would do just as well."

"Oh, that's not so bad." There was a pause for thought, and then: "Atkinson's got a golden syrup tin."

"There you are, then. It'd be just the job."

"I doubt if you'd hear much through it, though," Darbishire went on. "You see, it's still half-full of golden syrup. Of course, if we could wait till he's eaten it . . ."

"Well, we can't wait. When I get a supersonic brain-wave I like to get cracking straight away," Jennings said with rising enthusiasm. "After all, there must be hundreds of empty tins knocking about the school. For instance . . ." He broke off and searched his mind for a likely source of raw material. "I know! Mr. Carter always has round tobacco tins. He's bound to let us have some empty ones. Let's go along to the staff room and ask him."

So saying, he leaped to his feet and swept the scattered possessions back into his desk in an untidy heap.

"It's a pity you haven't got the telephone rigged up already," Darbishire remarked as he watched his friend's vain efforts to cram down the lid. "Then you could ring Mr. Carter up from here."

Jennings gave him a look. "That's just what *I* said a few moments ago, and you said I needed my brains testing," he replied. "Anyway, you're the crazy one now, because if we'd got our telephone rigged up already we shouldn't *need* Mr. Carter's tobacco tins."

"No, I didn't mean that. I thought you wanted to ask him about your English book."

"Oh, that!" Jennings lifted the desk lid once more and pushed the top layer of books into some semblance of order. As he did so, he noticed the English book for which he had been searching. But by now it didn't seem to matter. He was far too absorbed in his new interest to bother about an exercise book, or even to remember why he had wanted it in the first place.

At a brisk pace he led the way out of the classroom and along the corridor. As he turned a corner he almost collided with Binns and Blotwell, the youngest boys in the school, who were blocking the passage from side to side.

With his hands extended before him, Blotwell was making concertina movements with a loop of cotton upon which a cardboard disc was threaded. At each jerk of his hands, the disc spun round and round in a manner which gave the operator and his assistant intense satisfaction.

"Hey, Jennings, look at our new wheeze, copyright reserved," shrilled Binns at the top of his penetrating voice. "Blotters and I are the first chaps to be the only ones to invent ye famous spinning machine. I bet this will catch on like a house on fire when the other chaps see it."

Jennings favoured Binns with a pitying smile. "Tut, tut! Little things please little minds," he said indulgently. "Still, we can't expect much from Form One-ers, can we, Darbi?"

Blotwell ceased twirling his loop of cotton and bridled indignantly at this slur on what he seemed to consider was one of the greatest inventions of the twentieth century. "All very well for you to talk," he said. "I'd jolly well like to see you think of something better."

"You won't have long to wait," Darbishire retorted. "We've got an electronic brainwave lined up already. All we need are some empty tins."

A wary look came into Blotwell's eyes. "Empty tins of *what*?" he demanded suspiciously.

Jennings tapped the side of his head in a pitying manner. "You're mad," he announced. "What are empty tins usually full of?"

"Nothing."

"There you are then—that proves it!" Jennings turned and hurried away along the corridor. As he went he called back over his shoulder: "And you can put your famous craze in the wastepaper basket. Nobody will touch it with a barge-pole when they find out what Darbi and I are going to do."

As they pattered down the main staircase to the staff

room on the ground floor, Jennings' mind was busy planning further developments to his scheme. His first idea had been to construct a single telephone line solely for the novelty of such a proceeding. After all, a gadget which would enable a few chosen friends to send messages to one another was clearly a useful possession. But when the news began to spread other people might want to avail themselves of this valuable device, and would be quick to follow the fashion he had set. In no time at all the whole of Form 3—perhaps, even, the whole school— would be making their own instruments. In his mind's eye, he could picture the scene of bustling activity as the craze took hold: the common room festooned from end to end with cats' cradles of humming string as secret messages and other vital information sped from tobacco tin to tobacco tin.

By this time they had reached the staff room where they found Mr. Carter seated at the table preparing his lessons for the afternoon.

Jennings came straight to the point. "Sir, please, sir, have you any empty tobacco tins we could have, please, sir?"

Mr. Carter nodded. "Plenty. What do you want them for?"

"A famous scheme of mine, sir. I'll tell you about it if you like, sir."

Mr. Carter listened patiently. Fifteen years' experience of dealing with boys had taught the senior assistant master a great deal about the workings of the growing mind. For this reason he was respected by the boys in his charge who looked upon him as an ally who would always do his best to understand their point of view. At the same time, it was well-known at Linbury Court that Mr. Carter was a man who stood no nonsense. He had, moreover, a flair for seeing through deeply-laid plots, and any attempts to deceive him always ended in failure.

"All right, Jennings, I'll let you have some tins," he said when the boy had outlined his needs. "Not that I altogether approve of this project of yours. Wouldn't it

10

be better to devote your free time to something useful and worthwhile?"

"Oh, but it *is* worthwhile, sir. It's a new idea, you see . . ."

"New!" Mr. Carter raised a questioning eyebrow. "It's as old as the hills. This passion for home-made telephones crops up every few years with monotonous regularity."

"Well, new to us, anyway, sir," Jennings amended. "Actually, I thought the masters would be jolly pleased, really. You see, we shan't make nearly so much noise in the common room as we usually do because we shall be whispering into our tins instead of shouting across the room, sir."

"That's one consolation," Mr. Carter conceded. "But why do you have to whisper? Won't it work if you speak normally?"

"Oh, yes, sir, it'll work just the same, but we shall have to keep our voices down in case the person we're talking to hears what we say without using his earphone, sir."

Mr. Carter smiled to himself as he opened the cupboard door and searched for the all-important materials. It seemed to him that if a conversation could be carried on more easily by normal means there was little point in using the home-made device at all. However, it was useless to expect the self-styled telephone engineer to appreciate the force of this argument, so without further comment he presented him with a couple of empty tobacco tins, and was rewarded with a spate of thanks and beaming smiles of gratitude.

"Jolly decent of Sir, wasn't it!" Darbishire remarked as he followed his friend into the corridor and closed the staff room door. "They'll make supersonic hearing aids."

"They're *not* hearing aids—they're sensitive earphones," Jennings replied sternly.

"Well, you know what I mean. The point is they're just the right size for people with ordinary ears. I doubt if they'll fit your great elephant flaps, though."

"Well, I like the cheek of that!" Jennings protested. To prove that there was no truth in the slander he screwed a tin firmly over each ear. To his delight they fitted per-

11

fectly and remained in position without the support of his hands. He trotted along the corridor with the two tins sticking out from his head at right angles like a pair of handlebars.

There was no time, then, to complete the construction of the telephone, for the bell for afternoon school was ringing as the boys arrived back in their classroom. But after prep that evening they hurried away to the common room, the focal point of most of their out-of-school activities. Here, the seventy-nine boarders of Linbury Court could enjoy themselves in a large and pleasant room furnished with ping-pong tables, cupboards filled with a variety of indoor games, and the boys' own lockers overflowing with a wide assortment of private possessions.

Jennings and Darbishire lost no time in setting to work, helped and hampered by a group of third form boys who gathered round so closely that the two craftsmen had difficulty in assembling their apparatus.

"Hey, stand back for goodness' sake, and leave things alone!" Jennings protested as Temple and Atkinson, two eleven-year-old colleagues, pressed forward inquisitively. "How do you think Darbi and I can fix up a piece of delicate electronic apparatus with you two breathing down the backs of our necks like a couple of high-pressure air brakes?"

"Sorry," Temple apologised. "We only wanted to see how it works." He shifted his weight slightly, causing the throng about him to lose its balance and surge forward like a collapsing rugger scrum. When order was restored Jennings once more set about his task of threading the ends of a length of twine through the holes pierced in the bottom of each tin. Then he secured each end with a knot and turned to the crowd about him with a broad grin of triumph.

"There you are! Ye famous patent hi-fi intercom. walkie-talkie, all ready for testing," he declared. "The most supersonic invention ever known to science."

Atkinson expressed doubt. "I bet it doesn't work," he said. "Where are the batteries? Where's the electricity? Where are the high-fidelity microphones and things?"

12

"It doesn't need anything like that," Darbishire hastened to assure him. "According to Jennings the tin works like a drum, and if you keep the string tight the sound waves will make it vibrate."

"Look, I'll give you a demonstration," Jennings volunteered. He thrust one of the containers at Darbishire and marched off towards the common room door with the other tin in his hand. "I'll go right out of earshot—and out of eyeshot, too. You speak first, Darbi, and I'll answer."

So saying, the proud inventor hurried from the room. He'd show these sceptics whether his scheme was workable or not! He pulled the door to, leaving just enough room for the line to pass through. Then he applied his ear to the tin, screwing up his face in an expression of extreme concentration. Time passed, but no sound was audible in the earphone.

The door opened, and Temple's head popped out. "Darbi wants to know if you're ready yet."

"Of course I'm ready!" Jennings replied impatiently. "I've been standing here with my ears out on strings for the last hour and a half. Tell him to get a move on!"

After a short interval a crackling buzz sounded in the earphone. Jennings' face lit up and he flapped his free hand in the air in a wave of elation. Darbishire had made contact! . . . The gadget really worked! . . . Success! Success!

For the first few seconds the earnest listener had difficulty in making sense of the buzzing noises resounding inside the tin. *"Awah oojah inky bam,"* Darbishire seemed to be saying. Surely it couldn't be that!

After some moments, however, his ear became attuned to the rhythm; the distortion faded and to his delight he found he could hear with comparative ease.

". . . five elevens are fifty-five and five twelves are sixty," came over the line in tones which clearly belonged to Darbishire. Indeed, it was impossible to mistake his voice, for he had a habit of stressing certain syllables which gave the impression that he was speaking in capital letters. The voice continued: "Let's think. What else is there? Oh, yes! *The Brook*, by Alfred Lord Tennyson.

'I come from haunts of coot and hern,
    I make a sudden sally
And . . .'

Go away, Atki, you're putting me off!

'And sparkle something something fern
    To rumpty tumpty valley.'

Okay, Jen, it's your turn now."

Jennings removed his earphones and thought for a moment before replying. What should he say? Something scientific, perhaps, would be in keeping with the importance of the occasion.

He would be a space pilot, he decided; the first man ever to land on the moon, sending back vital information to his earthbound colleagues. He jerked the line taut and spoke into the mouthpiece in crisp, official tones.

"Hallo, Earth! . . . Hallo, Earth! Moon calling Earth. This is Space Pilot Jennings speaking from Lunar Base Camp One. Are you receiving me? . . . Are you receiving me? . . . Over!"

A faint voice from the Earth buzzed in the tobacco tin informing him that he was coming over loud and clear. How was he getting on up there? the voice inquired. Was the weather seasonable for the time of year?

"Lunar Operation proceeding according to plan," Jennings replied. "Actually it's a bit breezy around these parts. I'm jolly glad I'm wearing my fleecy-lined space suit. Our next move is to explore a handful of craters by moonlight, so stand by for the next news bulletin. Meanwhile here is a gramophone record of important history dates, specially requested by L. P. Wilkins, Esq., of Linbury Court School. . . ."

The master on duty that evening was Mr. Wilkins. He was a large man with a booming voice, a heavy footstep and a limited supply of patience. The fact that he was kind-hearted by nature was not always apparent, for he lacked the insight into the growing mind possessed by his colleague, Mr. Carter. As a result he was often at a loss to understand the behaviour of the rising generation. Try as he would, he could see no glimmer of common sense in many of the antics they chose to perform and which, to his way of thinking, were not merely bewildering but completely beyond the bounds of reason.

As he made his way along the corridor on his tour of duty, Mr. Wilkins caught sight of a familiar figure talking to himself outside the common room door. That in itself was not remarkable—queerer things had been known to happen at Linbury Court School; but as the boy was mumbling his monologue into a tin, the master on duty felt that some explanation was called for.

"What are you chattering away to yourself for, Jennings?" he demanded as he approached.

"Oh, I wasn't sir," the boy replied. "I was talking to somebody down on the Earth, sir—er—I mean, somebody in the common room."

The closed door seemed to cast some doubt on this statement, so he hastened to explain. "Actually, sir, I was transmitting a message by walkie-talkie—from the Moon, sir. You can hear them answer if you listen through this earphone, sir."

But Mr. Wilkins was not keen to know how things were going down on Earth. He looked upon most new crazes as time-wasting pursuits, especially those involving so-called operations in outer space.

There were reasons for this. Mr. Wilkins' dislike of imaginary space travel could be traced back to the embarrassing occasion when—purely by accident—Jennings and Darbishire had locked the school's most distinguished Old Boy in the library during a game of lunar exploration.*

*See "According To Jennings."

15

From that day onwards Mr. Wilkins had looked upon space travel with misgivings, and would always register a protest at any garglings, splutterings and throat-clearings which went on outside the door of his room when he was looking forward to a few moments of quiet repose. It was useless to point out to him that inter-planetary rockets have powerful engines which can only be imitated by making *wumph-wumph* noises with the full force of the lungs. The plain truth was that Mr. Wilkins was not space-minded, and that was that!

"Another of these ridiculous crazes!" he said in disapproving tones. "It beats me why you silly little boys have to waste your time fiddling about with nonsensical gadgets instead of doing something intelligent."

Jennings was mildly shocked at this description of his latest hobby. Surely Mr. Wilkins ought to know that the purpose of peaceful scientific inventions was to benefit mankind and spread knowledge and understanding throughout the world. Admittedly, the home-made telephone was not as important, in this respect, as X-rays or radio telescopes, for instance; but at least it was a step in the right direction. It was not easy to put all this into words, but Jennings did his best.

"Well, you see, sir, I'm only *pretending* this is a powerful radio transmitter, sir, but if it was a real one I should be able to do a whole lot of useful things with it, sir."

Mr. Wilkins looked doubtful. "Such as?"

"Well, sir, like, say, for instance broadcasting messages of peace and goodwill, and—er—all that sort of thing, sir. I mean, supposing there really *were* people on Mars and the Moon and places, sir—and there might be, for all we know—then we should be able to tell them we wanted to be friendly and weren't going to attack them or anything."

"No doubt," said Mr. Wilkins, shortly. "But for a start I suggest you leave the Martians to their own devices, and try spreading a little of this peace, goodwill and brotherly understanding amongst the members of Form 3. When you've got *them* to behave like civilised human beings you can start worrying about the inhabitants of outer

16

space, and not before."

"Yes, sir."

"And what's more, Jennings," Mr. Wilkins went on.
"I'm warning you that if this ridiculous make-believe of
yours leads to trouble, as it did last time, I'll—I'll . . ."
He searched his mind for a fitting punishment. Somewhat
lamely he finished up: "Well, it had better *not* lead to
trouble, that's all."

CHAPTER 2

JENNINGS MAKES HIS MARK

JENNINGS was not unduly worried by Mr. Wilkins' warning. He knew from past experience that masters often
expressed disapproval of out-of-school projects by utter-
ing vague threats which they had no intention of carrying out. And indeed it was difficult to see how a hobby
which was neither noisy, messy nor destructive, could
possibly involve anyone in trouble of any sort. Obviously, then, he decided, Mr. Wilkins did not really mean
what he said.

By the time the dormitory bell rang half an hour later,
the boys had concluded a series of tests which proved
that the home-made telephone was a fairly reliable instrument for sending messages any distance up to about
ten yards. They retired to bed well satisfied with the
success of their experiments.

The next morning Jennings and Darbishire spent
every moment of their free time with ears or mouth glued
to a tobacco tin exchanging pointless remarks about the
weather or inquiring after each other's health. By lunch
time the novelty was beginning to wear thin.

"You know, Darbi, we ought to think of something
else we could do with our walkie-talkie," Jennings remarked as he churned up the jam in his rice pudding
until his plate was a delicate shade of rose pink. "It's a

bit feeble you saying, 'How are you getting on?' and me saying, 'I'm all right. How are you?' over and over again."

Darbishire nodded absently. Just at the moment he seemed more interested in the patterns being formed on his neighbour's plate. Why couldn't Matron provide different sorts of jam—greengage, apricot and blackcurrant, for instance, he wondered. Then you could stir up your rice pudding into all the colours of the rainbow. With an effort he forced his mind back to the subject under discussion. "Yes, I see what you mean," he agreed. "Still, it's jolly difficult to know what else to say after the first half hour or so."

"Perhaps we could make up a game of some sort," Jennings suggested. "For instance, I could be a police car, and Atkinson or Venables or someone could be a gang of bandits who've just robbed a bank, and you could be the control room at Scotland Yard giving me instructions about which way they were escaping, and telling me where to go to head them off."

"Yes, but you couldn't actually *go* anywhere," Darbishire objected. "Not unless you left your walkie-talkie behind, and then you wouldn't be in touch with the control room any more."

"No, I suppose not. Well, never mind, I expect I'll think of something."

A plan to make the telephone unit more mobile occurred to Jennings shortly before the end of break the following morning as he and Darbishire were sitting on the common room window-sill making adjustments to their apparatus.

Down below on the quad, they could see Venables, a gangling, untidy boy of twelve, floundering round the asphalt on a pair of roller skates. His flailing arms and unsteady balance revealed that he was no skilful performer; but this was natural enough for it was only after breakfast that morning that the skates—a present from an uncle—had arrived by the parcel post.

"Wow! Look at old Venables lurching about like a bull on a bicycle!" Darbishire exclaimed as the skater,

18

unable to control his movements, ran full-tilt into a group of boys who had gathered to watch his antics.

"Give him a chance; he's only a learner," Jennings pointed out. "As soon as he's got the hang of it he'll be able to go zooming about fast enough to . . ." He broke off as a bright thought floated into his mind. "You know, Darbi, that's the one way the police car could move about without losing touch with Scotland Yard."

Darbishire wrinkled his nose in perplexity. He had forgotten about the conversation during lunch the previous day.

"If Venables will lend me his skates, that is," Jennings explained. "You could stand in the middle of the quad transmitting messages, while I go belting around on the other end of the string."

"You couldn't go very far," Darbishire pointed out. "It's only about ten yards fully stretched."

"Yes, but I could go round and round in a circle, don't you see. That would give me double the distance to start with, and I could keep on as long as I liked without stopping."

Darbishire was not impressed with this plan for improving the mobility of the flying squad, which seemed to him to be somewhat limited in scope. It was all very well for Jennings to go skating about at the full length of his tether, but this meant that the control room would have to spin round like a capstan to keep up with him, and the pivoting officer in charge would soon be too giddy to carry out his duties. It was useless, of course, to expect Jennings to appreciate this, so Darbishire decided to try a different line of argument.

"You'd have to be an expert skater to do it properly," he said. "A fine sort of mobile policeman you'd make if you kept sitting down every three yards."

"I *can* skate—well, a bit, anyway," Jennings retorted. "I learned last holidays."

"Yes, but can you do *fancy* skating? Figures of eight and all that?"

"No, not on rollers, you coot. That's a different kind

19

of skating altogether. You need ice and stuff for that sort of thing."

"So what? You can have pantomimes on ice, so why not roller skating on ice, as well?"

"Because . . . because . . . Oh, come on, let's go and ask Venables if he'll let me have a go."

They hurried out on to the quad, Jennings in the lead and shouting at the top of his voice to attract Venables' attention. But by now the skater had achieved a surprising turn of speed and was encircling the asphalt so fast that he was quite unable to obey the summons to halt.

"Can't stop!" he shouted as he flashed past. "You'll have to wait till I run down."

After three more circuits his pace slackened and he wobbled unsteadily to rest in Jennings' arms.

"Shall we dance?" Jennings inquired facetiously as Venables clutched him round the waist and grabbed his wrist for support. Gently, he freed himself from the embrace, and said: "I wanted to ask if you'd very decently let me have a bash on your skates."

"Well, I like the cheek of that! I thought it was something important. I wouldn't have stopped otherwise," Venables replied warmly.

"It *is* important. It's all to do with our telephone you see, and I must have a pair of skates to carry out the full treatment."

"I don't see why you should. You never lend me anything of yours."

"Oh, I will, honestly. I'll lend you . . ." Jennings racked his brains for an acceptable offering. "I'll let you have a go on the telephone afterwards."

"That's no good. I'm going to make one of my own."

"Well, I'll lend you my snorkel."

"I've got one already."

"Ah, yes, but yours is one of those weedy, feeble inner-tube efforts that keep going flat. I'll lend you my super-sonic garden-hose model *and* my torch, too."

"It's just the job for reading after lights out," Darbishire chimed in persuasively. "The best way is to go head first down the bed and get someone to tuck you in so you don't get a ghostly glow of light shimmering through the blankets. Then you can trail the snorkel out over the foot of the bed and . . ."

"I'll think about it," said Venables. "But you'll have to wait a week or two. I'm not lending my skates to anyone while they're new."

Jennings turned away, disappointed. What was the good of a vague promise for a couple of weeks hence? It was *now* that he needed them, while the urge to experiment was strong within him.

The bell for school put an end to his musing and, slightly disgruntled, he followed Darbishire indoors and up the stairs to their classroom.

According to the time-table the lesson was geography; but Mr. Wilkins, who taught this subject to Form 3, had decided to spend the first ten minutes of the period in holding an inspection of books and equipment.

It was some time since he had carried out a check of this sort, and for the past fortnight he had been exasperated during nearly every lesson by the reported loss of text books and the disputed ownership of unmarked rulers.

"Come along now, you boys. Get out your books in all subjects and lay them on your desks," he ordered when the class had assembled.

Form 3 registered mild surprise. "*All* our books, sir? But it's geog, sir," Bromwich pointed out.

"You heard what I said. And as well as books I want to see your pens, pencils, rubbers, rulers, geometry sets —the lot."

"Is it an inspection, sir?" inquired Atkinson.

"Of course it's an inspection. You don't imagine I'm organising an exhibition, do you! I'm going to make quite sure that all property is clearly marked with the owner's name."

The classroom hummed with activity as desks were flung open and their contents piled up in top-heavy pyramids on desk lids and seats.

A book inspection was a welcome break in the routine, Form 3 decided. Not only was it a pleasant change from copying geography notes, but also it would give them an excuse for making a fair amount of noise. Provided they could think of a few delaying tactics and time-wasting questions, there was no reason why the inspection could not be made to last for the rest of the lesson.

Temple started the ball rolling by saying: "Sir, please, sir, what shall I do, sir? I haven't got my name on my algebra book, sir."

"Put it on at once then," came the curt reply.

Darbishire was the next to raise a pointless query. Holding aloft a fragment of a broken ruler, its edges serrated like a breadknife, he said: "Please sir, I've only got about two inches of my ruler left, sir."

"What about it?"

"Well, sir, my name's too long to go on all in one piece, sir, so will it be all right if I write *Darbi* on one side and *shire* on the other, sir?"

"I—I—*Doh!* Don't ask such stupid questions, you silly little boy!"

"But, sir, I was only thinking . . ."

"Well, don't think!" snapped Mr. Wilkins. "Now the first thing I want to do is to make a list of all boys who are short of stationery, so keep quiet and put your hands up if you need anything."

It took some while to complete the list owing to the boys' inability to make up their minds as to whether or not they really were in need of various items of equipment. For instance, should Rumbelow put his name down for a new atlas if he thought he had one already but had lent it to Venables who had lost it? . . . Did Mr. Wilkins think that Bromwich's French exercise book would last him for the rest of the term provided he drew narrower margins? . . . Was it all right for Martin-Jones to order a new pencil if the one in his possession was only one and three-quarter inches long?

When at last he had dealt with all the queries, and altered his list so many times that it was barely legible, Mr. Wilkin's patience was growing threadbare.

"I'm going along to the stationery cupboard to get these things for you," he announced brusquely. "While I'm gone you'd better make sure you've got your name on all your books and writing materials."

At the door he was halted by an urgent plea from Jennings.

"Sir, please, sir, how can I mark my bit of bungee, sir?"

"How can you mark *what*?"

"My india rubber, sir. You see, I tried putting my name on in pencil, sir, but it wears off every time I rub something out. And I can't use ink because it goes all blotchy and spoils the——"

"I can't be bothered with your troubles now," Mr. Wilkins broke in impatiently. "You'll just have to think of some way of marking it permanently. I'm not taking any excuses."

"But, sir——"

"Be quiet, Jennings, and get on with what I told you to do. I warn you that if I find anything of yours that hasn't got your name on when I get back, I'll—I'll . . . Well, it had better *have* your name on, that's all!"

For some moments after the door had slammed behind Mr. Wilkins, Jennings sat pondering the problem that faced him. All his other possessions bore his name in bold capitals, but a satisfactory method of marking his rubber defeated him. Still, it would have to be done somehow, for now that he had drawn attention to the omission Mr. Wilkins would certainly want to know whether his orders had been carried out. . . . Should he carve his name with a penknife? Or bore a hole through the rubber and attach a tie-on label? As he toyed with these possibilities his eye strayed to a desk in the row in front of him where Bromwich was assembling his books for the inspection. Beside the pile lay a ruler upon which the owner had, on some previous occasion, branded the letters of his name by focusing the rays of the sun through a magnifying glass.

Here was the answer, Jennings decided. Here was a permanent method of marking which, in addition, gave him an excuse to conduct an interesting experiment.

Although it was late in the year, a recent spell of fine

23

weather had brought with it all the warmth of an Indian Summer. That morning in particular the sun was shining brightly. From his desk next to the window Jennings glanced up at the sky. Yes, it should be possible to use a burning-glass to good effect.

"Hey, Bromo, will you lend me your magnifying glass?" he asked.

Bromwich passed the glass back over his shoulder without comment, and at once Jennings set to work focusing the rays of the sun into a pinpoint of light directed on to his rubber.

He would have to keep the lettering small, he told himself, frowning with concentration as he held the glass steady. He would do a medium-sized *J* and a small *ennings*. With luck there would still be room for a full stop at the end. Mr. Wilkins would appreciate that: he was inclined to be fussy about correct punctuation.

The sunlight flashed on the magnifying glass and became a small white dot on the surface of the eraser. Presently a faint wisp of smoke curled upwards as the rubber smouldered in the concentrated heat. Jennings' eyes sparkled in triumph .. It worked! It worked!

Very slowly he began to move the glass, tracing out the first letter of his name. So absorbed was he in his handiwork that he had no thought to spare for the consequences. Indeed, he was not even aware that his experiment was producing an effect in the atmosphere around him.

Soon the wisp of smoke grew a little thicker and a smell of scorching rubber was wafted across the room.

From his desk in the front row Venables sniffed the air and turned to Temple seated beside him.

"I say, can you smell something burning?" he asked.

"I should jolly well think I can. Smells like rubber to me. Burning bungee. Phew!" Temple swivelled round seeking the source of the pungent aroma.

He soon found it! "Hey, Jennings, what d'you think you're doing? Trying to suffocate the whole form?"

Jennings looked up, surprised. "I'm only putting my name on my bit of bungee. Why, can you smell it over there?"

"I'll say we can. It's so chronic we can hardly breathe for the fumes."

"Don't worry. I've nearly finished. I've only got to do another . . ." Jennings broke off in alarm as the wisp suddenly turned into a spiral of smoke. "Hey! Help! The whole bungee's alight!" he cried, making frantic jabs at the smouldering object.

In a matter of moments the situation was under control, but by that time the air around his desk was dense with acrid fumes, and even in the farthest corners of the room the pollution of the atmosphere was becoming noticeable.

"Tut! It's all your fault, Temple!" Jennings stormed angrily. "If you hadn't made me look up while I was watching it, I should have seen what was happening.'

"Well, I like the cheek of that!" Temple defended himself. "If it wasn't for me we should all be gasping for breath and passing out by now."

"You must be crazy, Jen," Venables snorted. "Goodness knows what Old Wilkie will say when . . ."

The door swung open and Mr. Wilkins, carrying a pile of books and stationery, marched briskly into the room.

He didn't march far. After three steps he stopped dead in his tracks and sniffed the air like a well-trained bloodhound.

"I—I . . . Good heavens! There's something on fire in here!"

"It's quite all right, honestly, sir," Jennings hastened to assure him.

"It certainly isn't all right. I can smell it." Mr. Wilkins inhaled deeply to prove the truth of his observation. "Smouldering rubber, that's what it is."

"Yes, I know, sir, but it was an accident, you see. I was only doing what you told me."

"I never told you to set fire to the building."

"No, I mean about having everything marked, sir. I was just putting my name on my rubber, sir."

"What! With a burning-glass!" Mr. Wilkins' voice

25

"The whole bungee's alight!" he cried.

rose to a squawk of protest as his eye fell upon the tell-tale object lying on the desk.

"Yes, sir. It worked all right on Bromwich's ruler, sir, so I thought . . ."

"Doh! You silly little boy!" Dropping the pile of books on to the master's desk with a loud thump, Mr. Wilkins threw both hands above his head and marked time as though taking part in a primitive tribal dance. "Jennings—as usual! It *would* be! I never heard such fantastic tomfoolery! Making bonfires out of india rubbers! Filling the room with horrible fumes! Sending out dense clouds as thick as Red Indian smoke signals!"

It must be admitted that Mr. Wilkins' description of the conditions prevailing in Form 3 classroom was somewhat exaggerated. In point of fact, little now remained of Jenning's ill-fated experiment but an unpleasant aroma. It was, however, enough to provide the rest of the class with an excuse for staging a pantomime of bogus suffering.

"Wow! Coo! Phew! It's terribly thick over here, sir!" Venables complained, fanning the air with an exercise book.

"Yes, sir. We're almost suffocating," gasped Temple. "Can't we have some more windows open before we all get overcome and have to be carried out on stretchers, sir?"

As Form 3 awoke to the possibilities of the situation, a fusillade of coughing, choking and spluttering broke out on all sides of the room. With his handkerchief masking the lower half of his face, Atkinson staggered from his desk and fanned the polluted air out on to the landing by swinging the door vigorously to and fro. Bromwich gave a passable imitation of a man collapsing from lack of oxygen, while Rumbelow fastened a paper clip over his nose and applied artificial respiration to Martin-Jones.

"Silence! Stop this nonsense at once and get back to your places!" Mr. Wilkins ordered.

"But, sir, we can't breathe, sir," said Venables. "You said yourself that the whole room was . . ."

27

"Never mind what I said. Do as you're told and sit down in silence!"

When order was restored Mr. Wilkins said: "I shall keep the whole of this form in for extra work after prep this evening. . . ."

"Oh, sir!" came the chorus of dismay.

". . . *if* I have any more trouble from you this lesson."

Form 3 breathed again, grateful for the reprieve. Old Wilkie wasn't such a bad old stick really, they said to themselves.

"As for you, Jennings," the old stick went on, "I shall, in any case, set you a couple of hours' work to be done in detention on Saturday afternoon. Perhaps that will make you think twice before starting a poisonous conflagration another time."

Jennings felt aggrieved. "But I was only doing what you told me, sir," he protested. "You said I was to put my name on . . ."

"Don't argue with me, boy!" Mr. Wilkins thundered at the top of his powerful voice. "I've had just about enough nonsense from you, and if I have any more I'll— I'll . . . Well, there'd better not *be* any more nonsense, that's all!"

For some seconds he stood glaring at the unhappy occupant of the desk by the window. Then his anger faded and in more restrained tones he addressed the rest of the class. "And now, perhaps, we can proceed with the book inspection."

CHAPTER 3

TROUBLE AFTER DARK

WHEN Mr. Wilkins reached the staff room shortly after the end of morning school, he found one of his colleagues already installed in the armchair in which he had been hoping to relax. The occupant was Mr. Hind, a tall, dark-

28

haired man with a quiet voice and a look of patient resignation on his pale thin features. In out-of-school hours,
the curly stem of a short cherrywood pipe was for ever
clutched between his teeth, the bowl resting on the point
of his chin like a little wooden beard. His chief occupa-
tion was teaching art and music, but as this did not take
up the whole of his working day he filled in the blank
spaces on his time-table by teaching a few subjects to
junior forms. He glanced up as Mr. Wilkins entered the
room and noted that his colleague's brisk and bustling
manner seemed to have deserted him.

"What's the matter, Wilkins? Why the worried frown
and look of strain?" he asked.

"Huh!" You'd have a worried look, Hind, if you'd
wasted a whole lesson coping with Form 3's stationery
inspection," Mr. Wilkins replied with feeling. "Take that
boy Jennings, for instance . . ."

"Ah, yes! Jennings—as usual—it always is," said Mr.
Hind sadly, shifting his pipe from one side of his mouth
to the other. "He turned up for a music lesson the other
day with his fingers so plastered with congealed toffee
that he would have stuck to the keyboard if I'd let him
touch the piano."

"What can you do with a boy like that?" Mr. Wilkins
demanded, perching himself uncomfortably on a corner
of the staff room table. "I'm sick and tired of handing
out punishments."

"It isn't that he *means* to be disobedient; in fact, the
harder he tries to be helpful the worse turmoil he
creates." Mr. Hind scratched his long thin nose as he
pondered the problem. Then he said: "Perhaps we're
going the wrong way about it; perhaps, instead of
punishing him, we should give him more encouragement
so that he . . ."

"Encouragement!" Mr. Wilkins shot off the table in
horrified protest. "You don't expect me to *encourage* him
to start evil-smelling bonfires all over the building, do
you!"

"No, no, of course not. I was merely wondering . . ."
Mr. Hind sighed and shook his head. "Oh, well, never

mind. We can only hope that he will learn to see the error of his ways."

Unfortunately, Mr. Hind's hopes were not fulfilled; not, at any rate, in the week that followed. For it was on the ensuing Wednesday that Jennings found himself involved in further trouble owing to an unfortunate misunderstanding with the master on duty.

It was the home-made telephone that was really to blame. Now that Jennings had pioneered the craze, the urge to make similar instruments for themselves spread rapidly through the lower forms of the school. Binns and Blotwell organised the *Form I Telephone Exchange* and spent most of their free time surrounded by a pyramid of tobacco tins each bearing the name of a member of their form. In theory, one could call up the Exchange and ask to speak to another subscriber seated in a different part of the room; but in spite of some ingenious attempts to connect the two lines by joining a couple of tins together with elastic bands, no coherent message was ever known to get through.

As usual, Jennings took the lead in devising new ways in which the latest project could be used to best advantage. So far the only setback had been Venables' refusal to part with his cherished roller skates; and as he still seemed reluctant to co-operate a week later, Jennings abandoned this scheme in favour of one which promised to yield even more spectacular results.

"It came to me suddenly in the middle of maths prep," he announced to a chosen group of third formers whom he had summoned to a special meeting in the tuck box room to hear the details of the new plan. "What I thought was, how would it be if we fixed up a direct line between Dormitory 6 and Dormitory 4 for sending messages after lights out?"

"Good scheme!" Darbishire approved. "You'd let the line down out of the window, I suppose?"

"That's the idea." Jennings turned to Martin-Jones and Rumbelow, both keen telephonists, who were seated beside him on the hot water pipes. "That's where you two

30

come in. You'll have to be in charge of operations on the lower deck."

Jennings' plan depended on the fact that the window of Dormitory 4, on the top floor of the building, was directly above that of Dormitory 6 on the storey below. In the upper room slept Jennings and Darbishire together with Venables, Atkinson, Temple and Bromwich. The lower dormitory was much larger, and accommodated more than a dozen boys, including Martin-Jones and Rumbelow who slept one each side of the window.

When silence had been called and the dormitory lights were out, Jennings explained, he would lower one end of the telephone out of the upper window to the floor below. A slight tap on the pane would warn Rumbelow and Martin-Jones that operations were about to begin. Whereupon they would raise the cash and retrieve their end of the equipment from the sill.

"Old Wilkie, or whoever it is, will put our light out first and then stonk down to do the same in your dorm," continued Jennings, who was well-informed about the habits of masters on duty. "I'll be on the lookout, of course, and as soon as your window goes dark I'll know it's safe to get cracking on ye famous plan."

Rumbelow, podgy, red-haired and freckled, creased his brows in a puzzled frown. "Yes, I understand that part of it all right," he said. "But what sort of information are we going to send each other? There's no point in transmitting messages unless they're *about* something."

Although he was reluctant to admit it, Jennings knew that Rumbelow had raised a somewhat thorny problem. Experiments had already proved that after the thrill of establishing contact with a distant tobacco tin had worn off, it became more and more difficult to think of anything to say. But surely this was a minor snag! What mattered far more were the carefully-planned preparations, the veil of secrecy which surrounded the project and the excitement of being able to communicate under novel and difficult conditions.

"We'll soon think of something to talk about," he said airily. "For instance, you could—er—you could ring up

31

and ask for a time check; and we could say 'At the third pip it will be eight twenty-seven precisely'."

"Bags I do the pips," said Darbishire. With his hands cupped to form a tunnel from mouth to ear he practised sending out time signals to himself, alternately booming and squeaking *pip* noises on different notes of the scale.

What else could they do? Jennings wondered. So far, the most interesting messages had been those which he and Darbishire had devised during their so-called lunar exploration. Perhaps they could adapt the game to suit this new development.

"I tell you what, then," he said, turning to Rumbelow. "Dormitory 4 can be Mars or somewhere, and we'll pretend that you and Martin-Jones are down on Earth."

"Not much pretending about that," Rumbelow objected. "We've been down on Earth all our lives so far."

"Well, you know what I mean. Darbi and I are out in space and you two are our radio link recording all the data we send back."

"Oh, all right," said Martin-Jones grudgingly. "All the same, I don't see why we have to stay. . . ."

"Stop moaning and don't argue; it's all settled," Jennings broke in. "You know the drill. When you hear a zonking noise on your dorm window after lights out, you'll know that's the telephone being lowered into position. It's ever so simple, really."

"H'm! That's what *you* say," said Martin-Jones, who was somewhat pessimistic by nature. "We'll do our share, of course, but don't blame us if anything goes wrong."

"But I've just told you, there's nothing to *go* wrong," Jennings persisted. "It's a perfectly watertight wheeze."

Martin-Jones shook his head dubiously. "I've met your watertight wheezes before, Jennings," he said. "More often than not they come unstuck at the seams."

In the light of what happened later on that day, his doubts were fully justified.

Encouraged by Rumbelow and Martin-Jones, the members of Dormitory 6 undressed in record time that evening.

"Hurry up into bed, you chaps," Rumbelow urged his colleagues as they came into the room. "Mr. Wilkins is on dorm. duty to-night, and we don't want to keep him waiting."

"Why not?" they wanted to know.

"Because we've got a scheme laid on with Dorm 4. There's a message from Mars or somewhere coming over the blower after lights out, and we've got to get Sir out of the way first."

"So don't keep him talking when he comes in to call silence," Martin-Jones advised. "Just say 'good night' and let it go at that."

Mr. Wilkins was somewhat surprised when he reached Dormitory 6 shortly afterwards to find all the boys lying quietly in bed waiting for him to put out the light. Such an occurrence was most unusual, particularly as he had noticed the same readiness for slumber in Dormitory 4 which he had visited a few minutes earlier. He felt flattered by this respect for his authority. Obviously, the boys had come to realise that they had to be on their best behaviour when the master on duty was L. P. Wilkins, Esq.

He turned off the light.

"Good night sir. . . . Good night," said Rumbelow, even before the master's hand had left the switch.

"What do you mean, 'Good night'? I haven't gone yet."

"No, but you're just going, aren't you, sir?"

"I'll go when I'm ready, and not before," Mr. Wilkins retorted with dignity. "I like to make sure that everyone is settling off to sleep before I go downstairs." He strolled over to the window and stood for some moments looking down at the quad bathed in moonlight.

Martin-Jones grew anxious. Now that the dormitory light was out, the tell-tale signal would be sounding against the window-pane at any moment. "You don't *have* to stay in here specially for us, sir," he pointed out.

"That's all right. I'm in no hurry," said Mr. Wilkins. He turned away from the window and paced the room with slow, deliberate strides.

Thirty anxious seconds ticked past. . . . The situation was desperate. Rumbelow racked his brains for some reason to persuade the duty master to take his leave.

"I *thought* I heard the bell go for staff supper just then, sir," he said without much conviction.

"Did you indeed! Your sense of hearing must be particularly acute, Rumbelow . . ."

"Oh, yes, sir; it is; sir."

". . . if you can hear sounds before they actually happen. The bell's not due for a couple of minutes yet. You'll be telling me next that you can hear . . ." Mr. Wilkins paused as a sudden sharp tap sounded on the window behind him. He swung round sharply. "What was that?"

Dormitory 6 appeared to be struck with a sudden deafness.

"What was *what*, sir?" they inquired.

"Didn't you hear anything just then? . . . Not even *you*, Rumbelow, with your remarkable powers of hearing?"

Once more the knocking sounded on the pane.

"There it is again—a tap," said Mr. Wilkins hurrying back to the window to investigate.

"Yes, I expect that's what it is, sir. The hot one on the far wash-basin often makes a funny noise, sir," Martin-Jones suggested brightly. "It needs a new washer, or something."

"No, no, no. Not a *water* tap, you silly little boy. Someone is tapping on the window." So saying, the master on duty threw up the sash and thrust his head out into the cool evening air.

Jennings was nearly caught off his guard; but in the nick of time he saw that the head belonged not to Rumbelow but to Mr. Wilkins, and quickly hauled the line up out of harm's way. It was as well that he did so, for after straining his eyes downwards for some moments, Mr. Wilkins looked left and right and finally squinted into the gloom above his head in a vain endeavour to trace the source of the mysterious sound. Baffled, he withdrew his head and shut the window. "It's too dark to see properly," he grumbled. "I'm going outside to make sure that all's well."

He strode from the room and hurried down the stairs, determined to solve the mystery at all costs. In the hall he met Mr. Carter, to whom he confided his suspicions.

"I say, Carter, there's something funny going on outside on the quad," he began. "Someone's outside knocking on Dormitory 6 window."

Mr. Carter smiled his disbelief. "Nonsense, Wilkins. No one could reach that window from down below without using a ladder."

"All right, all right. I'm just telling you what happened. I'm not trying to explain it." Mr. Wilkins retorted. "Perhaps he *did* use a ladder, for all I know. The noise I heard could easily have been made by a ladder bumping against the glass."

"You suggest that some member of the domestic staff has had a sudden urge to clean windows by moonlight. Well, really, Wilkins! "

"Of course not. I merely said I've a suspicion that someone may be lurking about on the quad. Someone who took cover pretty quickly when I looked out. It might even be a burglar for all I know."

Mr. Carter refused to take the suggestion seriously. "I doubt it. It's extremely unlikely that a burglar would choose to break in at a time or place like this."

His colleague's disbelieving attitude did nothing to assuage Mr. Wilkins' ruffled feelings. In fact, he almost hoped that there *was* an unlawful intruder in the school grounds, if only for the sake of proving that, for once, Mr. Carter was in the wrong.

"I didn't say there *was* a burglar: I said there *might* be," he replied coldly. "And I should be failing in my duty if I didn't go outside and make sure."

"Right. I'll come with you," Mr. Carter volunteered with a slight smile. "I just can't wait to catch this mysterious evil-doer in the act."

The two masters slipped quietly out through the front door, closing it behind them so that the light from the hall should not betray their whereabouts.

It was cold outside, and Mr. Carter buttoned his jacket against the wind as he led the way down the steps. Then for some minutes the two masters searched the quad and crept furtively round the garages and bicycle shed in quest of an intruder. Needless to say, the search was fruitless.

"You must have scared him away when you poked your head out of the window," Mr. Carter observed drily as they paused on the edge of the playing fields.

Mr. Wilkins rounded on his companion with some heat. "You don't think there ever *was* a burglar, do you! You think I imagined the whole thing."

"I certainly think you were mistaken, though I agree you were quite right to come out and make sure. However, as there's obviously no one trying to force an entry, I suggest we go back indoors and have our supper."

It was not until they reached the front door again that they found that neither of them had a latch key. Mr. Wilkins tut-tutted in exasperation as he rang the bell. Having so carefully closed the door behind them they would now have to cool their heels on the doorstep in the chilly November air until someone arrived to let them in.

Half a minute later he rang the bell again; after that he knocked and rang several times but no one came to answer their summons. This was not really surprising, for by now most of the domestic staff had gone off duty and the other masters were out of earshot in the dining hall at the far end of the building.

"Let's try the side door," Mr. Carter suggested.

"That's no good. I went round and locked up just before I started dormitory duty," Mr. Wilkins said irritably. "This is ridiculous. We may have to go on waiting here until . . ."

He broke off, struck with a bright thought. While locking up, he had noticed that a window in classroom 2 had a broken latch and would not fasten properly. As this room was on the ground floor, it would be quicker if he were to climb in that way rather than wait any longer for someone to open the front door.

"It's all right, Carter. I've just remembered where

36

there's a window open," he went on with evident relief. "You stop here while I climb in, and I'll come round and open the door for you." So saying, he hurried down the steps, turned to the right past the flower-beds and was soon lost to sight round the corner of the building.

Classroom 2 faced the quad at right angles to the dormitory block. The outside wall was bathed in moonlight as Mr. Wilkins reached the window and fumbled to raise the sash. To his delight it opened easily, and a moment later he was kneeling on the window-ledge, his head and shoulders in the darkened room and his feet still dangling over the outside sill.

He would have been surprised had he known with what interest his movements were being watched from the window of Dormitory 4!

CHAPTER 4

FALSE ALARM

It had come as a great shock to Jennings some fifteen minutes earlier, to see Mr. Wilkins' head emerging from the window of Dormitory 6. . . . What had gone wrong? . . . Had Rumbelow failed them? . . . Had the plot been discovered? . . .

For a split second he had panicked, and in his confusion had nearly dropped the telephone on to the neatly-brushed head fifteen feet below. Fortunately, he had managed to regain control both of his feelings and of his apparatus, and had hauled the equipment to safety while the master on duty was still peering down at the quad.

Badly rattled, Jennings shut the window and reported the unexpected development to Darbishire in a hoarse whisper. "Wow! I thought I'd had it that time, Darbi. Sir's still in there."

"Fossilised fish-hooks! Are you sure?"

"Of course I'm sure. I nearly scored a direct hit *slap*

37

bang wallop on the target area when he poked his head out."

Darbishire was appalled at this disastrous turn of events. "Golly! You don't think he suspected anything, do you?"

"Oh, no, he didn't see me. I expect he just wanted a breath of fresh air, or something. All the same, we'd better wait a few minutes to give him time to go downstairs before we try again."

The dormitory linoleum was cold to the feet, and the two boys were thankful to climb back into bed to spend the time of waiting. From across the room came worried whispers from Venables and Temple demanding to know details of the hitch that had occurred. They were assured that the crisis had passed and that normal service would be resumed as soon as possible.

Darbishire snuggled farther down his bed and drew his knees up against his chest. The prospect of having to get out of bed again and stand around in front of an open window did not appeal to him at all, and he would have been only too pleased if the whole project had been cancelled.

Not so Jennings! "We ought to think out our messages while we're waiting," he suggested. "Then we'll be all ready to get cracking when the coast's clear."

"I can't see that it matters much," Darbishire replied without enthusiasm. He spoke in low tones, fearful lest his voice should be audible in the room below. "Anyway, for a start you could ask them why Sir hung around gazing at the moon instead of going down to his supper like a civilised human being."

"Yes, but what are we going to talk about after that?" Jennings persisted. "We've just landed on Mars, you see, and we've got to tell them all about it back on Earth."

"Well, why not say, 'Just arrived. Having a lovely time. Wish you were here'."

Jennings clicked his tongue in reproach. "We can't say that. You make it sound as though we'd popped over on a day trip and were sending a postcard home."

"Well, you think of something better then."

38

"That's what I'm trying to do!" Jennings retorted. "You don't seem to realise that the first space pilots to land on another planet will be making history, so we've got to send back a really supersonic and stirring message to the waiting world. Something like—well, something special and important that'll make everyone feel proud of our famous exploits."

There was silence in the dormitory as they wrestled with the problem of composing a message suitable for such an historic occasion. The home-made telephone was, after all, an instrument designed to promote peace and goodwill between Earthmen and planet-dwellers, Jennings reflected. In fact, he remembered stressing this point when explaining his hobby to Mr. Wilkins a few days earlier.

"I know what," he said at length. "Let's say, 'This is the International Inter-Planetary Expedition broadcasting the latest bulletin on 41.5 megacycles. . . .'"

Darbishire raised his head from his pillow. It sounded a promising start.

". . . We landed safely on Mars about tea-time, since when we have achieved many famous exploits for the sake of peace, goodwill and—and . . ." What was the phrase Mr. Wilkins had used when the purpose of the device was being explained to him? . . . Ah, yes, brotherly understanding, that was it.

". . . for the sake of peace, goodwill and brotherly understanding between Martians and Human Beings!" Jennings announced proudly. After a pause he added: "That is the end of the news summary."

"Just the job!" Darbishire agreed. "That ought to make Rumbelow and Co. scratch their heads a bit to think of a decent answer."

From his bed by the door Venables said: "Good job you're sending it by walkie-talkie and not by telegram. If you had to fork out three pence a word for all that lot you wouldn't have any pocket money left by the time you got back to Earth."

Jennings ignored the comment. "I should think Old Wilkie must have gone downstairs by now," he observed. "I'm going to have another bash at making contact." He

A man was climbing through the window.

scrambled out of bed and began to untwist the tangled length of string on the window-sill. "Wake up, Darbi. Don't just lie there; come and help me," he commanded.

Unwillingly, the right-hand-man obeyed. He put on his dressing-grown and slippers (it was jolly cold on Mars, he reminded himself), and pattered round the foot of the bed to assist his leader.

At that moment Jennings glanced through the window and saw a sight that made him catch his breath in astonishment. . . . *Down below on the quad, a man was climbing through the window of Classroom 2.*

"Petrified paint-pots! Look, Darbi, look!"

Darbishire followed the direction of his friend's pointing finger. "Wow! Who on earth is it?" he breathed.

They strained their eyes into the gloom but it was impossible to identify the shadowy figure at such a distance. One thing, however, was obvious: no law-abiding person would force an entry after dark in such a stealthy fashion.

Darbishire gulped slightly and whispered: "Do you think it's a burglar?"

"Must be," Jennings reasoned. "He wouldn't go crawling through the window at this time of night if he'd just popped in to inspect the gas meter, would he?"

"What had we better do, then?"

"We'll go and warn Old Wilkie. All the masters will be having supper by now, so they won't have heard this chap breaking in."

From these snatches of whispered conversation, the other occupants of the dormitory deduced that something sensational was afoot. Leaping from their beds they skidded across the linoleum to the window to find out what was happening. . . . They were just in time to see a pair of feet disappearing over the sill of Classroom 2.

Dormitory 4 throbbed with excitement. The home-made telephone was forgotten. All the make-believe of interplanetary expeditions vanished in the light of this startling development. For here was a real-life adventure such as seldom happened in well-regulated preparatory schools.

Jennings, as usual, took command. "Darbi and I will go downstairs and give the alarm. You other chaps stay

41

here and keep an eye on the quad in case he makes a bolt for it," he ordered.

Darbishire twisted his dressing-gown cord in an agony of apprehension. "Yes, but look here," he demurred. "Supposing we . . ."

"Oh, come on, Darbi! Don't stand there nattering!" Jennings broke in as he struggled into his dressing-gown and slippers. "We'll go straight down to the dining hall and tell one of the masters."

"Yes, but—wait a minute. I—er—I've dropped my glasses."

"You don't need your glasses. Just follow me and do what I say."

Seizing Darbishire by the arm, Jennings hustled him out of the room. Then, on tiptoe, he led the way down two flights of stairs to the lower landing. Outside the library he paused: below them was the hall which they would have to cross to reach the masters at supper at the far end of the building. Supposing they met the burglar face to face before they could summon help. Supposing . . . He stiffened as he heard a sound from below! Someone was moving about in the entrance hall.

Darbishire, too, had heard the sound and was registering symptoms of panic and alarm. With a gesture of caution Jennings edged forward and peered through the banisters.

"Can you see anyone?" Darbishire mouthed at him in a voiceless whisper.

Jennings nodded. . . . He could see Mr. Carter and Mr. Wilkins disappearing down the corridor on their way to the dining hall.

"Sir! . . . Sir!" he called softly. Too softly as it happened, for neither of the master heard him. Yet he dared not call more loudly for fear that the burglar was lurking within earshot: the only thing to do was to catch the masters up before announcing his news. With this in mind he signalled to Darbishire and together they tiptoed down to the ground floor and hurried along the corridor in pursuit.

By now the masters were out of sight, and the boys'

efforts to catch them up were thwarted by Darbishire's long, trailing dressing-gown which threatened to trip him at every step. With mounting anxiety they pressed on with the chase, and as they turned the last corner of the corridor they caught a glimpse of Mr. Carter and Mr. Wilkins disappearing through the dining hall door.

"After them, quick! " Jennings commanded.

"Yes, but what if——?"

"Don't argue, Darbi! The thief may get away if we waste time."

As Jennings spoke, the dining hall door opened again and Mr. Pemberton-Oakes, the headmaster, came out into the corridor having just finished his evening meal.

The headmaster of Linbury Court was a tall man, past middle age, with thinning grey hair and a placid expression which seldom betrayed what was going on in his mind. Whatever he may have thought at finding two third form boys scampering about the passage after lights out, his features gave no indication of surprise.

"What are you boys doing out of bed?" he inquired coolly.

Jennings, however, was far from cool. "Oh, sir! sir! There's a burglar in the school, sir!" he gasped, as he rushed the few remaining yards to the dining hall door.

The headmaster received the news without any change of facial expression. "Nonsense," he replied.

"But there *is*, sir—honestly."

"Yes, that's quite right. We've actually seen him!" Holding his dressing-gown clear of his ankles like some crinolined dancer performing a minuet, Darbishire shuffled forward to confirm the news. "Only his back view of course, but there's no doubt that's what he was, because we saw him climbing in through the window, and so did all the other chaps in our dorm, sir."

"And he's roaming about the school somewhere at this very moment, so we thought we ought to come and tell someone, sir."

The headmaster was impressed by the boys' urgent tones and their obvious air of sincerity. Unaware of the

43

duty master's recent method of entry into the building, he decided that here was a matter which required investigating. "And where exactly is this man?" he asked.

"We don't know where he is *now*, sir. It was some minutes ago that we saw him," Jennings volunteered. "But we didn't meet him coming down the stairs so he's probably still on the ground floor somewhere, sir."

"All right; I'll attend to this."

To their bitter disappointment the two boys were sent back to their dormitory while the headmaster made his plans for a systematic search of the building. It was most unfair, Jennings confided to Darbishire, as they climbed the stairs, that they, who by rights should be basking in glory for having raised the alarm, should be bundled back to bed just as the situation was approaching its climax.

To make up for this shameful treatment they called in at each dormitory on their way up to the top floor and broadcast the news of their sensational discovery. By the time they reached their own room the whole school was wide awake and agog with excitement.

Meanwhile the headmaster had not been idle. Having dismissed Jennings and Darbishire, he hurried back to the dining hall where Mr. Carter and Mr. Wilkins were just starting their soup. Mr. Hind and one or two other masters who had already finished their meal were preparing to leave the table. They looked up as the headmaster's face appeared round the door.

"A slight emergency has arisen," he announced. "I have reason to believe that there may be—ah—an unlawful intruder at large within the building."

The masters rose to their feet in a body. Mr. Wilkins, in particular, seemed very much on the alert.

"There may be nothing in it, of course, but on occasions of this sort one cannot be too careful," Mr. Pemberton-Oakes went on, almost apologetically. "So I suggest that we carry out an immediate search. You come with me, Hind, and we'll comb the basement, and perhaps the rest of you will join up in pairs and commence operations at different vantage points."

So saying, Mr. Pemberton-Oakes withdrew and hurried away along the corridor followed by Mr. Hind, his pipe clenched between his teeth in a grip of grim determination.

Leaving their soup to congeal, Mr. Carter and Mr. Wilkins followed their colleagues out of the dining hall. In spite of the gravity of the situation, the master on duty was unable to conceal a note of triumph in his voice as he said: "There you are, Carter. I was right after all. Now you have the Head's word for it perhaps you'll believe me. In fact, if only you'd shown a little more co-operation when I told you about my suspicions we might have got the whole business settled by this time."

Mr. Carter did not reply. He was puzzled. He would have liked to know where the headmaster had obtained his information; but for the moment this was not possible, for Mr. Pemberton-Oakes had already disappeared and was prowling round the basement boot-lockers armed with a hockey stick. The only thing to do was to carry out his orders and proceed with the search.

They searched for nearly half an hour—upstairs, downstairs, in classrooms, common room, library, kitchens and gymnasium. In the junior dormitory, where excitement had reached fever pitch, Binns and Blotwell carried out their own unofficial hunt, peering under beds and into cupboards, and even opening the laundry baskets on the landing in the hope of finding the miscreant cowering within.

But the quest was vain; of the burglar there was no trace whatever.

It was after nine o'clock when the masters foregathered in the staff room to compare notes. Mr. Hind was already there when Mr. Carter entered the room, but Mr. Pemberton-Oakes was still outside examining the flower-beds by torchlight in the hope of discovering footprints.

"Tell me, Hind," Mr. Carter inquired. "Did the Head mention who or what put him on the track of this elusive criminal in the first place?"

"Oh, yes. Two of the boys reported seeing him break in," the music master replied between puffs at his cherrywood pipe. "One of them was Jennings, I believe."

"Jennings, as usual!" A suspicion that had been worrying Mr. Carter for the past thirty minutes now became a certainty. "Come along, Wilkins," he said briskly. "I suggest we go aloft to Dormitory 4 and settle this matter once and for all."

"I don't see that *they* can help us. They've already told the Head all they know," Mr. Wilkins replied. "If you ask me, the chap's made good his escape. He may be miles away by now."

"I don't think he's all that far off," Mr. Carter said solemnly as he led the way out of the staff room and up the stairs.

In Dormitory 4 the two masters were greeted with excited queries when Mr. Carter switched on the light.

"Sir, have you caught him, sir?" squawked Atkinson, bouncing up and down on his bed like a clown on a trampoline.

"If you haven't he must still be about, sir," shrilled Temple. "We all saw him, honestly, sir."

"Ah, yes, but I was the *first* to see him," Jennings claimed importantly. "I saw him actually breaking in, don't forget."

"Now we're coming to it," said Mr. Carter. "Exactly when and where did you see this happen, Jennings?"

"Just a few minutes after the light went out in Dormitory 6, sir. I happened to look down on the quad, and there was a man climbing in through the window of Classroom 2, sir."

"What!"

Mr. Wilkins uttered a cry of anguish and waved his arms as though conducting an invisible orchestra. *"Classroom* 2! . . . Classroom 2 *window*! But, you silly little boy, Jennings, that wasn't a burglar! . . . That was me climbing in because I hadn't got a latch key!"

Jennings caught his breath in dismay and Darbishire's hand shot up to his mouth in guilty realisation.

"Oh, my goodness, what a frantic bish! I'm awfully

46 .

sorry, sir," Jennings stammered.

"Sorry! So I should think!" fumed Mr. Wilkins. "Do you realise you've made me spend half an hour walking round the building looking for *myself*! To say nothing of . . ." Suddenly he broke off and a puzzled look came into his eyes. He turned to Mr. Carter and said: "Yes, but look here, if Jennings' burglar turns out to be me, that still doesn't account for the chap I heard when I was in Dormitory 6—that tapping noise I told you about."

Mr. Carter strolled across to the window. In the gangway next to Jennings' bed was a dressing-gown carefully arranged to conceal what lay beneath. Mr. Carter removed the dressing-gown and picked up two tobacco tins joined together by a long piece of string. "I think perhaps this sheds some light on the mysterious tapping," he said. "Isn't that so, Jennings?"

The boy twisted the corner of his sheet and looked away. Finally he mumbled: "Well, yes, I'm afraid that *was* me, sir. You see, I was letting my telephone down to make contact with Dormitory 6, only Mr. Wilkins looked out instead, sir."

Mr. Carter clicked his tongue in patient despair. "This is too ridiculous for words," he observed. "It means, Wilkins, that *your* burglar was Jennings; and *his* burglar was you. So far as the security of the school is concerned, the two criminals may be said to cancel each other out."

The explanation did nothing to soothe Mr. Wilkins' feelings. "Yes, yes, yes. But what on earth was the silly little boy playing at, dropping telephones out of windows after lights out?"

The reply came in a strained, hesitant voice.

"Well, sir, we were pretending we'd gone on a journey into space. We were on Mars, you see, and we wanted to send a message. . . ."

"Mars! . . . Space! . . . Of all the footling tom-foolery!" snorted the master on duty.

"And what was the message you were going to send?" Mr. Carter inquired.

Jennings took a deep breath and crossed his fingers under cover of the blankets. "Well, sir, it was just to tell

47

them that we were doing all these things for the sake of —of peace and goodwill and brotherly understanding, sir."

"*Doh!*" Mr. Wilkins clapped his hand to his brow and leaned heavily against the doorpost. When the power of speech returned he expressed his opinion of the project in a few well-chosen words.

"You must be off your head," he stormed. "You cause all this commotion for the sake of *peace*! . . . All this ill-feeling for the sake of *goodwill*! . . . And you ruin my supper and send me on a wild goose chase round the building looking for myself for the sake of *brotherly understanding*! I never heard such fantastic nonsense in my life!"

He relapsed into an angry muttering in which the words "peace," "goodwill" and "brotherly understanding" could be heard against a background of exasperated protest.

It was too late, Mr. Carter decided, to probe into the matter that night. So with a warning to Dormitory 4 that the episode would be dealt with more fully in the morning, he switched off the light and escorted the indignant duty master back to his stone-cold supper in the dining hall.

Jennings lay in the darkness brooding over the events of the past half-hour. It was a pity about the burglar, he told himself: for in the fuss and excitement of capturing a real, live housebreaker, none of the masters would have had time to bother about the telephone line. Now, of course, there would be trouble about *that*. It was most unjust, really, because any fair-minded person would agree that the whole thing was merely an unfortunate misunderstanding—the sort of mishap that might occur to anyone keen enough to take an interest in worlds beyond our own.

But would an Earth-bound character like Old Wilkie look at it in that light! Not he! . . . The man just wasn't space-minded, and there was nothing that anyone could do about it.

CHAPTER 5

MORNING MUSIC

THE affair of the bogus burglar was investigated by Mr. Pemberton-Oakes the following morning. To Jennings' surprise and relief, very little was said about the raising of the false alarm; but this, as it happened, was really due to Mr. Carter, who pointed out to the headmaster that the boys had acted with the best of intentions and had merely been doing their duty in reporting what they had seen.

On the other hand, the ill-fated attempt to connect two dormitories by home-made telephone after lights out was an obvious breach of school rules, and was dealt with accordingly: the boys concerned were punished, the apparatus was confiscated, and all similar equipment was banned throughout the school for an indefinite period.

In addition, Mr. Pemberton-Oakes made a decision which was destined to have some bearing on the events of the following fortnight.

"I think we should keep a more watchful eye on the dormitories to make sure this sort of thing doesn't happen again," he told the masters when the matter was under discussion in the staff room. "And with that in mind I have decided—as an experiment only—to make the senior boy in each dormitory responsible for good behaviour after lights out."

"That's all right so far as the older boys are concerned," Mr. Carter observed. "But in the middle and junior dormitories you may have difficulty in finding anyone who is reliable enough to be placed in charge."

Mr. Pemberton-Oakes conceded the point. "I don't propose to give these temporary monitors the same powers as full school prefects, of course," he explained. "Their job will be merely to see that school rules are obeyed

49

after lights out, and to report any irregularity to a member of the staff. Any boy of initiative should be able to do that."

The headmaster's gaze travelled round the table and came to rest upon Mr. Wilkins. "It will obviously help matters if the boys know that there is a master close at hand after they have gone to bed, and for this reason, Wilkins, I'm hoping that you won't mind changing your bedroom and moving nearer to the dormitory block."

Mr. Wilkins had no objections to offer. "Very well, H.M.," he agreed. "I suppose you want me to move in to the spare room next to the music room?"

The headmaster nodded. "Thank you, Wilkins. I'm sure you'll be very comfortable there. Mind you, when once the boys have settled down for the night I don't suppose you will be called upon, or indeed, put to any inconvenience. The mere knowledge that a master is in the vicinity will smooth the path of these newly-appointed monitors and ensure that discipline is maintained."

The list of dormitory captains appeared on the notice board that afternoon. In Dormitory 4 the choice fell upon Bromwich, whom the headmaster considered to be slightly more level-headed and dependable than the rest of his room-mates.

The new monitors carried out their duties with quiet efficiency, and during the fortnight that followed there was seldom an occasion to report any boy for disobeying dormitory rules.

Mr. Wilkins, too, was well-satisfied with the arrangements, for his new room was more spacious than his old accommodation in the west wing. Apart from taking an occasional stroll round the dormitories during the evening to see that all was well, he was not put to any trouble at all.

There was, however, one drawback to the new system which he had not foreseen. And this was the fact that only a thin wall of lath and plaster separated his comfortable quarters from the music room next door. The wall was by no means soundproof: and though all was quiet in the evenings, the early mornings were rendered hideous by jangling discords from boys practising in the adjoining room.

On the first morning he was awakened by the rising bell at a quarter past seven, and then relapsed into a peaceful doze from which he was rudely disturbed by an unmusical crash, as though someone had dropped a book on the keyboard. After a pause, a melody faintly recognisable as Beethoven's 'Minuet in G' came thumping through the wall, but after a few bars it petered out and was followed by a long silence. Then came a one-fingered rendering of 'God Save the Queen' played on the lowest octave of the piano.

Mr. Wilkins rose from his bed, crossed the room in two strides and knocked on the wall. The National Anthem ceased abruptly and was replaced by four bars of Beethoven. After that came a noise like a whirring carnival rattle which could only have been made by someone marking time very rapidly on the foot-pedals. This died away and was succeeded by a long silence. Finally, the one-fingered rendering of 'God Save the Queen' broke on the air once more.

The master tut-tutted in exasperation. Some silly little boy was wasting his time in no uncertain manner. Mr. Hind would have something to say when he learned how his carefully planned time-table of music practice was being carried out.

As soon as he was dressed, Mr. Wilkins strode purposefully into the adjoining room.

"Jennings, as usual!" he barked as his eye fell upon the occupant of the music stool. "What's going on in here?"

"Nothing, sir," the boy replied, startled by the master's sudden appearance. "At least, only me doing my practice, sir."

"And since when have you been taught to play the piano with one finger?"

"I was playing by ear, sir."

"Oh, were you!"

"Well, one ear and one finger, sir," Jennings amended. "You see, I got to a hard bit that Mr. Hind hasn't shown me yet, so I was just . . ."

"Now listen to me," Mr. Wilkins broke in. "If your music practice is from half-past seven until the breakfast bell goes, I want to hear you playing for the whole of that time without stopping."

"You *want* to! You mean you *like* my playing, sir? Is that why you knocked on the wall?"

Mr. Wilkins shuddered slightly. "That certainly wasn't *applause*, Jennings. And whether I like that tuneless thumping you call playing is neither here nor there. The point is that now my room is next door I can hear everything that goes on—and everything that *doesn't* go on, too."

"Yes, sir."

"So if you hear me knock on the wall, that's a warning to you to stop wasting your time and get on with your practice."

A worried look came into the pianist's eyes. "Well, sir, I have to stop sometimes, sir, to turn over, or when the loud pedal sticks, or when I'm not quite sure what the next note is."

52

"I'll make allowances," Mr. Wilkins returned curtly. "It so happens that I *can* tell the difference between a pause for turning over a page and a ten-minute break for staring out of the window." He turned to leave the room and paused on the threshold. "And if I have to knock on the wall more than once for that sort of nonsense, I'll—I'll—well, you'd better look out."

As the door shut behind Mr. Wilkins, Jennings turned back to the keyboard shaking his head sadly. In the past, the half-hour before breakfast had always been looked upon by the less gifted of Mr. Hind's pupils, as being by far and away the best time for practising the piano. For it meant that the task was over and done with in the early hours, leaving the rest of the day free for other pursuits. . . . But with Mr. Wilkins in the adjoining room goading the musicians on to greater and greater efforts, the early morning practice would lose much of its former attraction.

It was not that Jennings disliked learning music; indeed, he took a keen interest in his twice-weekly lesson with Mr. Hind and looked forward to the time when he would be a skilled performer. But that, of course, wouldn't be for some years yet, and in the meantime he was inclined to regard the daily practice as a piece of routine to be endured rather than enjoyed.

For two whole weeks he applied himself seriously to his work, mindful of the pounding on the wall that would start every time he stopped for a brief respite. And at the end of that time he was given a demonstration of the great gulf that still lay between his standard of performance and that of an accomplished pianist.

It happened during his Thursday morning piano lesson with Mr. Hind, when for nearly a quarter of an hour the music room had been re-echoing to a halting and jerky version of Beethoven's 'Minuet in G.' After a particularly resounding discord that set his teeth on edge, the music master laid a restraining hand on his pupil's arm.

"No, no, no, Jennings! That note is G, not F. You always make the same mistake when you get to this bar."

"Yes, I know, sir," the pianist apologised. "Shall I go

53

back to the beginning and have another bash, sir?"

Mr. Hind winced visibly. "Have another *what*, Jennings?"

"Sorry, sir. Er—another shot, I should say."

Patiently, and with great restraint, the master said: "Before you start again, Jennings, try to remember that the music is meant to be *played*: not bashed or shot or rattled off or cracked at, or anything else."

"Yes, sir."

"It sounds to me as though you haven't been practising properly."

"Oh, but I have, honestly, sir," Jennings protested. "You have to, with Mr. Wilkins next door. He always bangs on the wall if I stop to blow my nose or anything, and he's hardly had to knock for over a week."

"I'm delighted to hear it," Mr. Hind observed. "All right, Jennings, try the piece again."

This time the passage was repeated without the playing of any wrong notes, but the pauses were so prolonged as the pianist strove to find the right chords that the final result showed little improvement on what had gone before.

"There, sir! I got it right that time," Jennings announced triumphantly. "I reckon I've got it off pat now, sir. A bit more practice and I shall be able to rattle it off . . ."

"Jennings! "

"Sorry, sir. I mean I shall be able to *play* it really well, shan't I, sir?"

"H'm! " Mr. Hind stroked his nose thoughtfully. "Would you like to hear the 'Minuet in G' played properly?"

"But I *did* play it properly that time, sir."

"That's what *you* think! " Mr. Hind rose from his chair and made his way to the record player standing in one corner of the room beside the instruments of the Form 1 percussion band. "I've got a record of that piece by a very famous pianist, if you'd like to hear it."

"Coo, yes, rather, sir." Jennings jumped up from the piano stool and hurried across to help. He switched on the record player and opened the lid while Mr. Hind sorted through a cabinet of records of classical music until he found the disc he was looking for. Then they sat down and listened to the music.

From the opening bars Jennings was forced to admit that there was little resemblance between his version of the piece and that played by the pianist of international repute. . . . Wow! This old geezer's not bad, he reflected. In fact, he's jolly good. Of course, some music *does* sound better on a decent record player than on the wheezy old music room piano, and, anyway, the chap's probably had more practice than I have. All the same, I wish I could . . .

Mr. Hind interrupted the train of thought with a quiet word of advice. "Listen carefully. He's just coming to the passage that always gives you so much trouble."

Jennings nodded. Had the pianist felt nervous, he wondered, when approaching this somewhat tricky stage of the recording? Apparently not, for the notes flowed smoothly, without even the slightest of pauses to suggest that the performer was wondering which fingers to use for the difficult chords.

"Wacko! He got that bit right—first shot!" Jennings exclaimed. "He hasn't made a single bish so far, sir! " "

Mr. Hind suppressed a smile. "Amazing! " " he said.

When the record stopped, Jennings heaved a sigh. "I wish I could play the piano like that, sir."

"I'm sure you do," Mr. Hind replied as he closed the lid of the record player. "And I only hope that this record has been of some use in giving you an idea of what can be achieved."

"Oh, yes, sir, it has." The glib answer came automatically and without reflection. . . . For indeed it was not until later in the term that Jennings conceived the idea of putting the Beethoven record to really practical use.

CHAPTER 6

UNWELCOME PROMOTION

THE bell for mid-morning break was sounding as Jennings left the music room at the end of his lesson. On the way downstairs he was hailed by Venables who came trotting out of the common room with a roller skate dangling from each hand.

"Oh, there you are, Jen," he began. "Listen; do you still want to do that swop you asked me about? A loan of my skates for your torch and snorkel?"

Jennings was mildly surprised. So much time had elapsed since he had made the suggestion that he had almost forgotten about it.

"It's a bit late for that, now," he said, as memory returned. "The whole point of borrowing your skates was so I could use them with my telephone. And that's all off now telephones have been stopped."

"I don't see why," Venables persisted. "Skates are always decent things to have a go on. Unless of course you can't really skate after all and you were just swanking. . . ."

"Of course I can skate!"

"Okay, then, what about doing that swop? You can borrow them every day for a week in exchange for that book about great explorers you've got in your tuck box."

"Book?" Jennings' eyebrows rose inquiringly. "You just said you wanted my torch and my snorkel."

"And your book as well, of course. That's all part of the bargain. After all," Venables went on persuasively, "there's no point in borrowing all the equipment for reading under the bedclothes unless you've actually got something to read, is there?"

There must be more in this than met the eye, Jennings decided. On the face of it, it would surely be asking for trouble to attempt to read after lights out, now that each

56

dormitory had a monitor, alert and watchful, to maintain discipline when silence had been called.

"You're crazy," he said. "You'd never get away with it with Bromwich sleeping only two beds away. He's been as bossy as blinko ever since he was made dorm captain. He ticked Atkinson off for snoring the other night, and he even threatened to report old Darbi for talking in his sleep."

A smug, self-satisfied look spread over Venables' features. "Don't worry about that! There won't be any trouble from old Bromo, you mark my words."

"How d'you know?"

"Because he won't be there, that's why. He was feeling rotten at breakfast and when he reported to Matron she bundled him off to the sick room."

"What's the matter with him?"

"How should I know! 'Flu, mumps, measles, chicken pox—probably the lot," Venables replied unfeelingly. "Anyway, he's taken his pyjamas and things, so I don't suppose we'll see him again for a few days."

So this was the motive behind Venables' offer! Jennings stroked an imaginary beard as he turned over the proposition in his mind.

The reason why he had suggested the exchange in the first place did not, of course, apply any more. On the other hand, the prospect of skimming round the quad on the borrowed skates was one that appealed to him strongly. Besides, if Venables had devised a scheme for taking full advantage of the dormitory prefect's absence, who was he—J. C. T. Jennings—to interefere in an affair which did not really concern him?

"Well, all right," he said at length. "If you lend me your skates you can have my torch and my book on great explorers. but I can't see why you want the snorkel as well. If Bromo's in the san. you can read after lights out without bothering to go under the bedclothes."

"Yes, I *could*," Venables agreed. "But Old Wilkie may be prowling around, don't forget, and if he saw a light shining he'd go off like an H-bomb. So if you don't mind I'll borrow the whole works, just to be on the safe side."

There were still a few minutes left before the end of break, so Jennings decided to try his skill as a skater without delay.

"I'll let you have the torch and things later on," he said as he accompanied Venables out on to the quad. "I've got them all handy in my tuck box."

"Right-o. And you'll find the skates in my boot-locker whenever you want to borrow them. You'll have to come to me for the key, though. I keep that in my pocket to stop people from having a go without per."

Assisted by the owner, Jennings attached the skates to the soles of his shoes. Unlike some types which were held in position by straps, Venables' skates were fitted with an expanding metal toe-piece in the shape of a claw which held the shoe in a vice-like grip. A key was provided for opening and closing the toe-piece, and without this essential piece of equipment the skates could neither be attached to the wearer's feet, nor yet removed from them.

"Keep your great hoof steady while I screw it up," Venables commanded as Jennings fidgeted with impatience. In a matter of moments the skates were in position and he was rolling, somewhat unsteadly, on his first circuit of the quad.

Darbishire came up to watch his friend's progress. "Jolly good!" he acclaimed generously. "A bit more practice and you'll soon find your sea legs."

"You mean quad legs," Venables corrected.

"Same thing. Anyway, just give old Jen a chance and he'll be zig-zagging about like a guided missile."

After a few laps Jennings began to gain more confidence, but his balance was still rather unsteady and he had not really got into his stride by the time the bell sounded for the next lesson.

"I'll have another shot to-morrow," he said as Venables bent down to unscrew the skates from his feet. "I'm glad you suggested this swop, Ven. I reckon it's going to be jolly well worth it."

The mild bilious attack from which Bromwich was

suffering was mentioned in conversation in the masters' common room after lunch.

"Matron tells me that he'll be back in school in a day or so," Mr. Pemberton-Oakes remarked to some of the masters who had foregathered for a cup of coffee. "In the meantime, I'm wondering whether I ought to appoint another boy to take over his duties as dormitory captain."

Mr. Wilkins gave a grunt of dissent. "If you ask me, H.M., I'd say that apart from Bromwich there's no one in Dormitory 4 capable of being put in charge of a rabbit hutch, let alone a roomful of bouncing third-formers."

"Come, now, Wilkins, they're not as bad as all that," the headmaster replied. "Some of them may be a trifle— ah—high-spirited at times, I don't deny. All the same, this might be an excellent opportunity of find out whether any of them have the qualities of initiative and leadership that will stand them in good stead when they become senior boys themselves." He furrowed his brows in thought. "Now let me see, who is there to choose from?"

"There's Venables, of course," suggested Mr. Hind. "He's one of the eldest in that dormitory."

"A possible candidate; he might do very well," Mr. Pemberton-Oakes agreed. "Is there anyone else worthy of consideration?"

There was a short silence. Then, surprisingly, Mr. Carter said: "How about Jennings?"

Mr. Wilkins nearly dropped his coffee cup. *"Oh, no!"* he cried with a wail of anguish. "Spare us that, Carter— even as a joke."

"It wasn't meant as a joke," replied Mr. Carter. "But if the H.M. is looking for qualities of leadership he might think twice about Jennings. I don't guarantee he'd be a success, but he's more of a leader than all the others put together."

"Maybe he is, but *where* would he lead them!" remonstrated Mr. Wilkins. "He's about the worst behaved of the lot."

Somewhat to his own surprise, Mr. Pemberton-Oakes found himself supporting the view of his senior assistant.

"That's one very good reason why we might give him a trial," he observed. "I have often found in the past that the most difficult boys make the most efficient prefects. The very fact of being placed in charge seems to put them on their mettle. Isn't that so, Carter?"

"It is, indeed. Mind you, I shouldn't suggest Jennings if the job was likely to go on for any length of time; but as it's only for a day or two it might be a good chance of letting him find out for himself that being responsible for the good behaviour of other people is no easy matter."

"Yes, I dare say, but—*Jennings*! " Mr. Wilkins wrinkled his face in a grimace of disapproval. "I mean to say— well, dash it all. I *ask* you! "

For some minutes the headmaster sat pondering the matter in silence. It would be interesting to see how a boy like Jennings would tackle a job of this kind. It might be the making of him! It might help him to turn over a new leaf. On the other hand, the experiment might well end in chaos. . . . Perhaps it would be safer to choose Venables after all. It was a difficult matter to decide.

"I'll think it over during the afternoon," he said as he laid down his coffee cup and rose to leave the room. "In any case, I'll let you know my decision before tea."

When afternoon school was over Jennings hurried downstairs to the basement and unlocked his tuck box. From it he took his torch, his snorkel and his book. It was a jolly good book, too, he reflected, as he flipped open the cover and glanced at the inscription on the fly-leaf: *To John, with best wishes from Aunt Angela*. . . . Good old Aunt Angela! It was decent of her to send him such an exciting story. As soon as he started reading it, Venables was sure to be carried away by the description of life in the African jungle.

There was just one snag about that, though, Jennings thought, as he closed his tuck box and made his way upstairs: if Venables became *too* absorbed in the book he might use up all the torch battery before he fell asleep. Still, that was a risk that would have to be taken. The bargain was made and there could be no going back on it now.

In the common room he found Venables waiting for him. "Don't use too much battery, that's all," Jennings said grudgingly as he handed over his possessions.

Venables placed the articles in his locker and shut the door. "That's all right. I'll be careful. And you can have my skates any time you want them if you'll just . . ."

He broke off as the tall figure of Mr. Pemberton-Oakes appeared in the doorway and made his way into the room.

There was a silence as the headmaster subjected each boy in turn to a long and penetrating stare. It was as though he was wrestling with a problem and could not quite make up his mind.

Finally he said: "Jennings, come along to my study. I'd like a word with you."

As he followed the headmaster along the corridor, Jennings' mind was in a whirl of puzzled wonder. . . . What was the reason for this unusual summons? He had been on his best behaviour for the whole of the previous fortnight so it was unlikely that he was to be taken to task for some alleged misdeed.

Unless of course. . . . For a moment he wondered whether his transaction with Venables could have come to the ears of Mr. Pemberton-Oakes. But no, it couldn't be that, he assured himself, for the arrangements had been made in private and the equipment had been concealed in Venables' locker before the headmaster had made his appearance. What, then, lay behind it all?

He was not kept long in suspense.

"I think it is time, Jennings, that you began to develop a more serious attitude towards school life and learned to set an example to others," the headmaster began as he lowered himself into the armchair in his study. "So far this term you have not been doing that. Quite recently I had to speak to you for upsetting the smooth running of school routine with that ridiculous contraption which you were pleased to call a telephone."

"Yes, sir." The boy stared fixedly at a spot on the wallpaper just behind Mr. Pemberton-Oakes' left ear. Was this

just a vague lecture on behaviour in general, he wondered, or was the Head getting ready to launch an all-out
attack?

"And before that you created a disturbance in Mr.
Wilkins' class by causing a—ah—a particularly obnoxious
conflagration."

"A *what*, sir?"

"I am told that you set fire to your india rubber."

"Oh, I see. Well, yes, I did, in a way, sir, but it was
just an accident," Jennings explained. "You see, Bromwich put his name on his ruler with a magnifying glass,
so I thought . . ."

Mr. Pemberton-Oakes dismissed the explanation with
a wave of his hand. "Never mind the excuses, Jennings.
The fact remains that it's high time you pulled up your
socks and . . ."

The boy stooped to obey the command.

"No, no, no! Not in so many words. Leave your socks
alone and listen to me. Now, Jennings . . ." the headmaster paused and then went on in man-to-man tones
which he hoped would inspire confidence. "Now, Jennings, I am quite sure that if I were to give you an important and responsible job to do, you would carry it
out to the best of your ability."

"Oh, yes, sir. I'd try ever so hard, sir."

"Of course you would. And with that in mind I've decided to place you in a position of trust. I'm going to
put you in charge of Dormitory 4 while Bromwich is
away."

Jennings stared at the headmaster in dumbfounded
amazement. "*Me*, sir!" he gasped in incredulous tones.
"Me? . . . Dormitory *captain*, sir?"

"On trial only, mind, to show what you can do," the
headmaster added hastily.

"Yes, of course, sir. Only . . ." Jennings broke off and
twisted his fingers nervously. There seemed to be something preying on his mind.

"Well——?" prompted Mr. Pemberton-Oakes.

"Well, there's just one thing, sir. Could I start being

dormitory captain to-morrow instead of this evening, sir?"

A slight frown creased the headmaster's forehead. Had he, after all, made an error of judgment in selecting Jennings for a duty of this kind?

"My dear boy, you can't pick and choose over a serious matter like this," he pointed out gravely. "You must understand that this is an honour—a great responsibility."

"Yes, I know, sir," came the wavering reply. "But there's just one snag about starting straight away. You see, I—I . . . ." Again the words tailed off into an embarrassed silence.

He was in a hopeless situation, Jennings told himself. How could he explain to the Head that he had just agreed to help Venables to break the rules of the school (and *dormitory* rules at that!) which, as the newly appointed monitor, it would be his duty to enforce!

If only he had known about his appointment *earlier*! . . . . If only he had refused to listen to Venables' wretched offer. If only . . . .

He pulled himself together, aware that the headmaster was regarding him with a look of puzzled inquiry.

"It's all right, sir. I'll manage somehow," he mumbled.

"That's the spirit!" Mr. Pemberton-Oakes approved. "Right! Off you go, then. I'll see that the boys in your dormitory are informed of the new arrangements, and— ah—the best of luck, Jennings! I'm relying on you not to let me down."

The boy gulped and forced a wan, unhappy smile. "Thank you, sir," he said as he turned to the door.

CHAPTER 7

JENNINGS TAKES CHARGE

As he made his way back from the headmaster's study, Jennings wrestled with the problem that faced him. Having been chosen for a position of trust he must do his duty whatever the consequences. Perhaps there was still time to persuade Venables to cancel the agreement. At any rate, it was worth trying.

Accordingly, he hurried along to the common room where he found his fellow-conspirator glancing through the pages of the book which he was hoping to read later on that evening.

"Oh, there you are, Jen. What did the Archbeako want you for?" Venables demanded.

"He told me that I'd got to—er—that he'd decided to . . ." A sudden shyness, amounting to a feeling of self-conscious guilt swept over the temporary dormitory captain. It was as difficult to express his feelings now as it had been in the study five minutes earlier; for Venables would be sure to hoot with derisive laughter when he heard of the new appointment. Perhaps it would be better to say nothing about it until the news had been officially announced by one of the masters. Meantime, however, the ill-timed conspiracy must be scotched in no uncertain manner.

"Never mind about the Archbeako." There was a note of anxiety in Jennings' voice as he went on: "Listen, Ven; that swop we'd arranged to do—it's all off."

Venables' mouth dropped open in surprise. "What on earth are you woffling about?"

"I'm not going on with it. I've changed my mind. The deal's fallen through."

"It jolly well *hasn't* fallen through!" Venables retorted angrily. "What's the big idea?"

"I can't explain now, but I want my snorkel and things back right away."

"Oh, do you! Well, you're going to be unlucky. You should have thought of that *before* you borrowed my skates, not afterwards. If you think," Venables continued with growing resentment, "If you think that you can make a bargain and then back out of it when you've already had part of your share, then you can go and take a running jump at yourself."

"Yes, but don't you see . . ."

"You're a rotten chizzler, Jennings. You just wanted a
64

free go on my skates, and now you've had it you calmly turn round and tell me the deal's off!"

Jennings shook his head. "It's not like that at all, really," he insisted. "It's just that—that—well, I advise you to do what I say or you'll be sorry."

By way of reply Venables thrust the book back into his locker, slammed the door and turned the key. "It's no good your trying to threaten me," he observed as he made his way out of the room. "When I make a bargain I keep it—not like *some* people I could mention."

On his way up to bed that evening Darbishire called in at Matron's dispensary, seeking treatment for what turned out to be a purely imaginary chilblain. As a result he was the last to arrive in his dormitory where, to his surprise, he found most of his colleagues in a state of wild jubilation. No sooner had he crossed the threshold than Atkinson greeted him with a squawk of excitement.

"I say, Darbi, have you heard ye famous latest news bulletin?"

"No, I've been down to Matron. What's up?"

"Mr. Carter's just been in and told us. Well, you know old Bromo's been carted off to the sick room with bubonic plague or the Black Death, or something?" A slight exaggeration of the symptoms would, Atkinson felt, heighten the drama of the astounding news he was about to impart. "Well, who d'you think's been put in charge of the dorm in his place?"

Darbishire wrinkled his nose in thought. "Venables?" he hazarded.

"No! Guess again."

"Well, I know jolly well it wouldn't be *me*," Darbishire said emphatically. "How about Temple?"

Atkinson let out a cackle of maniacal laughter. "You're miles out! You'll never guess. It's Jennings!"

"Wow!" Darbishire's head jerked forward in surprise, causing his loosely-seated spectacles to bounce up and down on his nose. He swung round and beamed a smile of congratulation at his friend who was standing beside his bed looking extremely self-conscious and pretending not to notice the scenes of rejoicing going on in other parts of the room.

"Hearty congrats on your famous appointment, Jen," Darbishire said warmly. "I'm jolly pleased, actually."

Jennings muttered a sheepish word of thanks.

"We're *all* jolly pleased," Atkinson announced with glee. "Don't you see, Darbi, it means that we shall be able to do as we like now without being reported. We can talk after lights out . . ."

"Or read books," added Venables.

"Or have a pillow fight, or a dorm feast, even," suggested Temple.

"Oh, no, you jolly well won't! You've got to carry on just as though Bromo was here!"

The brusque interruption shattered the atmosphere of gleeful anticipation, and with one accord the boys swung round to see Jennings glowering at them in defiance.

For a moment there was silence. Then Temple's face lit up in a grin of understanding. "You're just trying to pull our legs," he decided.

"Of course he is," said Venables. "After all, there's no point in having him as dorm pre if we don't make the most of it." He favoured the monitor with a winning smile. "You wouldn't report us, would you, Jen? You wouldn't do a thing like that to your oldë and ancient comrades in arms?"

Never before had Jennings felt so disconcerted in the presence of his fellows. Now for the first time he found loyalty to his friends conflicting with his duty to authority. He was facing a situation which could be resolved only by taking a firm stand, even though it meant incurring the resentment of his colleagues.

"I didn't ask to be made dorm captain," he said gruffly. "But as the Head's picked on me I've jolly well got to do the job properly."

"Wow! Watch out, chaps, Jennings is on the warpath!" Temple said in accents of mock terror. "Please, Jennings, may I kindly have per to clean my teeth?"

"Please, Jennings, may I breathe?" Venables jeered.

Darbishire felt suddenly angry at this uncalled-for

criticism of his best friend. Who did Temple and Venables think they were to talk like that? "You needn't try to be funny," he said. "Old Jen's got quite enough on his plate without you two making it harder."

Venables and Temple exchanged glances of pained surprise.

"*We're* not being funny," said Temple. "Jennings is the one who's being funny, pretending he's going to throw his weight about and keep us in order."

"Hear, hear," added Atkinson. "After all, he's fooled about more than anyone in the past, so he can't very well expect us to obey him now."

"Yes, I dare say, but that was *before* I knew I was going to be dorm captain," Jennings defended himself. "It's all different now."

"Oh, well, if you're going to take *that* attitude . . ." Temple turned away with a shrug and his mood was reflected by Venables and Atkinson who started to undress in sullen silence.

Jennings heaved a sigh as he stooped down to unlace his shoes. For the first time he began to realise some of the difficulties which Bromwich had had to contend with. Being a monitor wasn't as easy as some people seemed to think.

The atmosphere was still heavy with resentment when Mr. Hind, who was on dormitory duty, came in ten minutes later to put out the light and call silence.

It was clear that Venables was not going to accept the new situation without a struggle. As the duty master's footsteps died away in the distance, he reached under his pillow for the torch and the book which he had brought with him up to the dormitory.

"I've got a jolly good book here, Temple," he remarked chattily. "Jennings lent it to me. It's all about a chap who meets another chap in the jungle and . . ."

"Quiet! Stop talking!" came the order from the bed by the window.

Venables affected to sound surprised. "Are you talking to me Jennings?"

"Yes, I am."

"Oh!" There was a short pause. Then, in a very marked manner, Venables went on with his conversation. "Well, anyway, Temple, these two chaps decide to go on an expedition to catch tigers. . ."

"Sounds pretty exciting. Bags I read it after you," said Temple, hoping to goad the dormitory captain into an argument.

"Shut up!" Jennings called sharply. "You've jolly well got to keep quiet when I tell you."

"Yes, that's right. Don't make a row, Temple," Venables observed blandly. "How do you think I can read my book with you nattering all the time!"

"There isn't going to be any reading—or any nattering, either!"

Venables clicked his teeth in reproach. "Honestly, Jen, you've got a nerve," he remarked, switching on the borrowed torch and sending its beam dancing on the ceiling. "Why, only the other night Bromo had to keep telling you . . ."

"All right, all right. You needn't bring that up," Jennings said uneasily.

The moment had come, Darbishire decided, to speak up on behalf of his friend. "Hear, hear! It's not Jen's fault he's been put in charge," he said. "He's got to carry out his orders, and it's not fair of you other chaps to go on talking when he tells you to stop."

"You're talking yourself now, Darbishire, so *you* can't talk!" Temple pointed out.

"Ah, yes, but I was only . . ."

"Oh, shut up, all of you!" Jennings shouted at the top of his voice. "And switch my torch off, Venables, or there'll be trouble."

Venables blew out his cheeks in aggrieved protest. "Well, I like the cheek of that! You lent it to me specially so I could read to-night, and what's more, you've already had a go on my skates in exchange. You can't go back on your word now. You promised."

A feeling of baffled frustration came over the dormitory prefect. Secretly, he couldn't blame Venables for insisting on his rights. And yet—and yet . . .

"Yes, but don't you see, I *wouldn't* have promised if I'd known what was going to happen," he blurted out.

"Jennings is right," Darbishire chimed in staunchly. "If he's been picked for the job he's got to do it."

Temple snorted. "There goes Darbishire, talking again and breaking the silence rule. Why don't you pick on *him*, Jennings?" he demanded. "Just because he's your friend you let him go on chuntering at the top of his voice; but if Venables or I happen to whisper a bit, you kick up no end of a hoo-hah."

The situation was getting out of hand, Jennings decided. The time had come for action. "Listen, Venables," he said. "If you don't switch off my torch and stop reading I shall confiscate it."

"He's bluffing," said Temple. "Fancy confiscating his own property. He must want his brains testing."

In the darkness the beam of the torch remained clearly visible. Obviously Venables had decided to call the bluff.

"I shall count three, and if you haven't switched it off by then I shall come over and take it," Jennings announced. "One . . . two . . ."

Venables turned a page and went on reading, and for a moment the dormitory prefect wavered. "I shall give you up to *five*," he amended, hoping to stave off the fateful moment. "Three . . . four . . . *five*."

With slow deliberation Jennings got out of bed and strode the length of the room Although it was dark he was conscious of the stir he was creating in the neighbouring beds and was aware that Temple, Atkinson and Darbishire were sitting bolt upright, agog with excitement.

By now he had reached the bed by the door. "Come on, Venables, hand over," he said quickly.

"No, I jolly well won't," came the defiant retort.

"Yes, you jolly well will!" As he spoke, Jennings' hand shot towards the book resting on the pillow. Venables made a movement to restrain him, dropping the torch and seizing his opponent by the wrist. Jennings broke away and snatched up the torch. By its light he saw his snorkel lying on the blanket at the foot of the bed. Venables saw it too, and both boys dived for its possession at the same instant.

There followed a tug-o'-war, Venables pulling on the length of hose with all his might while Jennings heaved and strained to wrest it from his grasp.

"Leave it alone, Jennings. You said I could have it," panted Venables.

"You do as you're told and don't argue," said the voice of authority.

By this time the other three occupants of the dormitory were kneeling on their beds shouting encouragement and advice.

"Go on, Venables, Don't let him have it!" urged Temple.

"Go it, Jen. Make him give it up!" shrilled Darbishire.

"Bash him up! Knock him down! Sit on his head!" cried Atkinson, who as a neutral was quite happy to encourage both sides in the hope of stimulating a really worthwhile contest. . . . The noise was deafening and the sound of the uproar travelled far beyond the walls of Dormitory 4.

At last Venables gave up the struggle. "Oh, all right, all *right*," he protested angrily, releasing hold of the snorkel. "Take the beastly thing. *And* your rotten book. *And* your rotten torch."

Gasping slightly, Jennings gathered up the confiscated possessions and started to move back to his bed.

"You're crazy to let him have them," said Temple. "He wouldn't have dared to report you."

"Well done, Jennings, well done!" cried Darbishire, heedless of the carrying powers of his penetrating voice. "Victory! Victory!"

"Oh, shut up, Darbishire!" Venables snapped irritably. "You and Jennings are as bad as each other. I wish to goodness I'd never borrowed his beastly things: I wish I'd never said he could have my skates. I wish . . ."

The dormitory door hurtled open and the light clicked on. Standing on the threshold was Mr. Pemberton-Oakes.

In a silence which could be felt the headmaster's gaze swept round the dormitory and came to rest upon the boy in charge standing guiltily in the middle of the room clutching a book, a torch and a length of garden hose fitted with a funnel at each end.

It has been said that M. W. B. Pemberton-Oakes, Esq., M.A. (Oxon.), was a man who never allowed his face to betray his feelings; and though the sight of his newly-appointed dormitory monitor rooted to the spot with shame and dismay came as a shock to him, his features showed no trace of anger or surprise.

For some seconds he remained staring at the woe-begone figure before him. Then he said: "What are you doing out of bed, Jennings?"

"Er—just getting into it, sir."

"So I observe," the headmaster replied. "And taking with you a torch, a book, and a—ah—a device obviously designed to enable you to read under the bedclothes."

"Oh, no, sir. At least, I mean . . ." Jennings shifted

71

from foot to foot. He could, of course, explain why he had the confiscated property in his possession; but that would mean implicating Venables, and he had no wish to do so if it could be avoided. He felt like a reformed burglar stopped by a policeman while in the act of dropping his housebreaking tools in the river.

"Is that your torch, Jennings?" the headmaster demanded.

"Yes, sir."

"And your book?"

"Yes, sir."

"And the piece of rubber tubing; do you deny that that is also your property?"

Jennings looked down at his feet and mumbled an affirmative. The circumstantial evidence against him was very strong indeed.

To Mr. Pemberton-Oakes the evidence was not merely strong: it was conclusive proof that the boy was taking advantage of his position as dormitory prefect to break the rules which he had been appointed to uphold. The headmaster was disappointed to think that his judgment had been so badly at fault. At the same time he was determined to be fair.

"Well, Jennings. I am waiting for an explanation," he said.

The boy's mind was in a whirl. Somewhere inside him there seemed to be a tug-o'-war going on between two conflicting loyalties. He could prove his innocence only at Venables' expense; yet to do this was unthinkable, for he himself had been a party to the crime when it was first suggested. To speak now would only make matters worse. He continued to look down at his feet, and said nothing.

It was natural that Mr. Pemberton-Oakes should interpret the silence as a confession of guilt. "So this is how you carry out your duties! You, of all people, Jennings!" He spoke in the tones of some medieval monarch unmasking a case of high treason. "I should never have believed that any boy in this school would so shamefully abuse a position of trust."

"Oh, but, sir. You don't understand . . ." Jennings faltered.

"I understand perfectly well. And I am dismayed to find that you would stoop to doing the very thing which I asked you to prevent. You should be ashamed of yourself, Jennings. I had faith in you. I chose you for a position of responsibility and you have let me down."

"Oh, but, sir. It wasn't like that at all, really. You see, I was only trying . . ."

"That's enough!" snapped the headmaster. "The facts are plain. You are no more fit to be in charge of this dormitory than—than . . ." His eyes swept round the room seeking a suitable simile. ". . . . than that wash-basin."

As he lay in bed listening to the tirade, Venables began to feel a qualm of conscience. After all, his conscience told him severely, it was hardly fair to let old Jennings take *all* the blame when he, G. Venables, was really the cause of the trouble. When his conscience had finished outlining the case, Venables spoke up.

"Sir, please, sir, it wasn't altogether his fault, sir. You see, what happened was . . ."

"Be quiet, Venables. I have no wish to hear any trumped-up excuses." Mr. Pemberton-Oakes thrust out his hand and took the three disputed articles from Jennings' grasp. Then he motioned to him to get back into bed. "You are no longer in charge of this dormitory, Jennings," he said. "I shall put someone else in your place." He glanced at the occupants of each bed seeking a suitable successor. "Let me see, now. Ah, yes, Venables."

"Yes, sir?"

"I shall appoint you temporary monitor in place of Jennings."

"Oh, *sir!*" Jennings was unable to restrain the cry of protest that welled up inside him at this new injustice. Venables, of all people! It wouldn't have been so bad if one of the others had been chosen—but *Venables*! That was the last straw!

The headmaster took no notice of the interruption. "You will be responsible for seeing that silence is observed after lights out. Can I trust you to do that?"

"I'll try, sir," Venables mumbled. He was acutely aware that his recent conduct had made him quite unworthy of his new position, and he carefully avoided catching the eye of his predecessor.

"At any rate, you could hardly do worse than the last boy I selected for this duty." Mr. Pemberton-Oakes remarked as he prepared to leave the room. "Now, there's not to be another sound from this dormitory to-night. I trust that's clearly understood."

The light clicked off and the door closed.

CHAPTER 8

TANGLED WEB

FOR some moments after the headmaster had left the room there was a tense, uneasy silence. Then Jennings' outraged feeling rose once more to the surface.

"Coo! Jolly well not fair! Jolly well not fair!" he protested.

"Hear, hear! Mouldy chizz!" Darbishire agreed in a hoarse whisper.

Somewhat self-consciously the new prefect strove to assert his authority. "Shut up talking, both of you!" he said.

"Well, I like the cheek of that!" Jennings burst out. "*You* telling *me* to shut up. It's jolly well not fair! '

To Atkinson the new situation seemed full of interesting possibilities. "I don't see that you've got anything to moan about, Jennings. You can get your own back now," he pointed out. "You've only got to make a row and the Archbeako will come prancing back and tick Venables off for not keeping you quiet . . ."

"Serve him jolly well right," said Darbishire.

". . . and then perhaps he'll make Temple dorm pre instead. And then someone else could kick up a hoo-hah and it'd be my turn to be put in charge. And after that

74

we could have Darbishire, and then we could start all over . . ."

"Be quiet, Atkinson!" commanded Venables.

"Oh, all right. I was only thinking how easy it would be. Jennings has only got to start . . ."

"Well, I'm not going to," Jennings broke in. "It's not so easy being dorm prefect as some people who haven't tried it seem to think."

"Hear, hear." This time the approval came from Venables. On this point, at any rate, he and Jennings were in complete agreement. "So shut up all of you, and let's go to sleep."

No further word was spoken until the rising bell sounded at quarter past seven the next morning. Then, while the boys were dressing, Darbishire rallied once more to the assistance of his friend.

"If you want to know what I think, Venables, I reckon you're a jolly rotter letting old Jen take the blame like that," he began as he weaved his way into his grey flannel shirt. "If you'd had any decency you'd have told the Head it was all your fault."

Venables shrugged. "So I would have done if he'd let me," he defended himself. "I tried to explain but he wouldn't give me a chance to get a word in edgeways."

"Well, why don't you go along to his study and tell him this morning, then?"

Venables stopped short in the act of pulling on his socks. His conscience was still worrying him and he was willing to go to some length to make amends. On the other hand, he could see no point in making the situation worse than it was already.

"It's too late to tell him now he's made me dorm pre," he reasoned. "After all, *I'm* supposed to set a good example."

Jennings nearly choked over his tooth mug. "Good example!" he spluttered. "You're just trying to get out of it. I had to take the blame when the Archbeako thought it was my fault."

"Yes, I know, but that was just bad luck. No point in raking all that up again," Venables put in hurriedly. He pulled on a garter and snapped it round his leg with a loud smack. "I tell you what, though, Jen. I'll be specially decent to you from now on, to make up for it."

"Coo, favouritism!" protested Temple. "I suppose you're going to let him read under the bedclothes."

"No, I shan't. We had enough of that caper last night," Venables replied thoughtfully. "No, I'll make up for it by—by . . ." He paused to search his mind for a generous offer. "Well, you can borrow my skates whenever you like. I can't say fairer than that, can I?"

Jennings snorted. "Huh! You owe me that anyway. You promised to lend them to me in exchange for my snorkel and things."

"Ah, yes, but that's all cancelled now. After all, it was you who backed out of that bargain, don't forget."

"Well, of course I did. I suppose you expect me to . . . Oh, what's the use of arguing. The damage is done now."

Distressed and angry, Jennings banged his tooth mug down hard on the washbasin. Then he screwed up his pyjama jacket in a tight ball and hurled it at Atkinson who was grinning at him in a fatuous and irritating manner.

It was time now for his music practice. Jennings struggled into his pullover and stalked off down the dormitory scowling at his colleagues in a manner that left them in no doubt about his feelings. As he reached the threshold he turned and blurted out: "It's all your fault, Venables. It's all because of you that the Head thinks I'm no good and he can't trust me any more. . . . And if you think you can get round me with a lot of flannel about mouldy roller skates, you're jolly well barking up the wrong tree."

The door slammed behind the unwilling martyr with a crash that set the toothbrushes rattling in their beakers.

Mr. Hind had often complained that Jennings played the piano without feeling and made little effort to capture the mood and expression which the music demanded. On this particular morning, however, there was no doubt that the piano was echoing the pianist's feelings; and in the adjoining room Mr. Wilkins winced and plugged his ears with his fingers as the sound of Beethoven's "Minuet in G" came thumping through the wall charged with every symptom of anger, bitterness and frustration that the suffering musician could express.

Mr. Carter noticed during breakfast that morning that Jennings had something on his mind. The boy's appetite had deserted him, and he sat staring moodily at his plate and taking no part in the lively chatter going on around him. Having heard from the headmaster of the events of the previous evening, he thought at first that the boy's mood was one of self-reproach—a natural feeling of guilt and shame at having failed to make good in his hour of trial. . . . And yet there seemed more to it than that, Mr. Carter decided: there was a smouldering resentment in his attitude towards the other members of his dormitory which became obvious whenever they tried to include him in the conversation. His hostility towards Venables, for example, seemed quite unreasonable in one who was solely to blame for his own misfortunes.

When the meal was over Mr. Carter strolled down-stairs to the basement. Experience told him that Jennings, wanting to be alone, would probably seek solitude in the tuck-box room where no one else was likely to be at that time of the morning. Sure enough, as he entered the room he saw a lonely figure perched on the hot-water pipes, his elbows on his knees and his chin cupped in his hands.

"You're looking very upset, Jennings. Are you worrying about that business in the dormitory last night?" Mr. Carter asked.

Jennings looked up quickly and then rose to his feet. How could Mr. Carter have known what he was think-ing? But then, he reminded himself, Mr. Carter always *did* know everything. Well, *nearly* everything! Still, it was unlikely that he was aware of the true facts behind the present disastrous misunderstanding.

Impulsively the boy burst out: "I don't think the Head was at all fair, sir."

Mr. Carter raised one eyebrow. "And was it fair of

you, Jennings, to take advantage of being a dormitory prefect to break school rules after lights out?"

"Oh, but I didn't, sir."

"I understood that the Head found the room in an uproar while you were fooling around out of bed with a torch and a book you'd brought up for reading after lights out."

Jennings twisted his fingers in a gesture of frustration. "Oh, but, sir, that's all wrong, honestly, sir. I wanted to explain to the Head but I couldn't think how to put it, and in any case he wasn't in the mood to listen, sir."

"Well, I'm listening," said Mr. Carter. "Try explaining to me."

It was a fair enough offer; but even so it was not easy for the boy to express all that he felt deep down inside him. What upset him most was not that he had been deprived of his position, but the thought of how low he had sunk in the headmaster's estimation: for it was obvious that Mr. Pemberton-Oakes believed the incident to have been a deliberate abuse of privilege by a boy in whom he had placed his trust.

But how could he explain this error of judgment, Jennings asked himself, without revealing the part played by Venables? Perhaps, if he was tactful, he could straighten out the muddle without mentioning names.

"Well, sir, I wasn't going to read after lights out," he began. "The reason why I got out of bed was to confiscate the torch to stop—er—to stop someone else from reading. And this person made a fuss, sir, and the Head came in just as I'd got the things away from—er—from this person, and he thought I was to blame."

Mr. Carter nodded. "Whereas, in point of fact, you were merely doing your duty?"

"Yes, sir. At least, I was trying to."

"I see," said Mr. Carter slowly. "Well, this puts things in rather a different light. If that's what really happened, I'll have a word with the headmaster on your behalf."

Jennings said: "Thank you, sir." His worried expression faded, and the wide-awake look came back into his eyes. Good old Mr. Carter, he thought. You could always

78

rely on him to look at things in a sensible way. . . . But his rejoicing came too soon.

"Yes, I think, perhaps, when the Head knows all the facts . . ." Mr. Carter was saying; and then he paused, and narrowed his brows in a frown of doubt. "Yes, but just a minute. This torch and these other things that you so zealously confiscated: whom did they belong to?"

"Well, actually—as a matter of fact—they were mine, sir."

"Indeed! And how did this other boy come to have them in his possession?"

Jennings shifted uncomfortably. They were approaching that point in the conversation which he had been anxious to avoid. To his way of thinking, his conduct had been understandable; but would a grown-up see things in the same light? With some reluctance he said: "Well, you see, sir, I'd agreed to lend these things to this other boy so that *he* could read."

Mr. Carter's right eyebrow, which had recently returned to its normal position, again rose a couple of centimetres. "Now we're getting to the root of the matter. It strikes me that the Head's judgment was right after all."

"Oh, *no*, sir," Jennings protested. "You see, I lent him my things *before* I knew the Head was going to make me dorm prefect."

"And you think that excuses your conduct?"

Jennings groaned inwardly. Surely Mr. Carter could appreciate that the whole argument depended upon this point. Everyone knew that it was inexcusable for a prefect to break the rules; but for an ordinary non-privileged person to do the same thing—well, he *shouldn't*, of course, but it was just one of those things that happen from time to time.

"Well, yes, I think it does, sir. You see, it was jolly awkward for me being put in charge just after I'd made all these arrangements," he explained. "So the only thing I could do to put matters right was to confiscate the things I'd just lent him, sir. And that's how the trouble started."

It is doubtful whether the logic of this argument

79

appealed to Mr. Carter as strongly as it did to Jennings. It was, however, clear that the boy was taking things very much to heart, and felt that his motives had been misunderstood.

"I shouldn't go on brooding about it," Mr. Carter advised. "You'd better go outside and get some fresh air before school starts."

The headmaster and Mr. Wilkins were standing by the notice board discussing matters of school routine when Mr. Carter reached the hall a few minutes later.

"Excuse me butting in, H.M.," he said as he joined them; "but I'd like to have a word with you about that business in Dormitory 4 last night. Jennings is taking it very badly and . . ."

"So he should be! I'm glad to hear that he has *some* sense of shame," Mr. Pemberton-Oakes observed.

"Yes, but it's not quite so simple as that." And Mr. Carter went on to explain the details leading up to the incident.

The headmaster was not impressed. "That doesn't excuse his conduct at all."

"No, I know it doesn't, but the boy thinks it does." Mr. Carter maintained. "He's all mixed up about it. He's feeling badly about letting you down; and he's feeling even worse because he thinks you've condemned him without knowing his side of the case."

Mr. Pemberton-Oakes pursed his lips and frowned.

"I don't see that any useful purpose will be served by re-opening the matter," he said. "In any case, Matron tells me that Bromwich will be back in school to-morrow, so the question of who can be trusted to take charge of the dormitory will no longer arise."

"Very well, H.M.," Mr. Carter agreed. "But I still think we might give Jennings another chance to make good, if only to show him that he's not being treated so badly as he seems to imagine. Any small job would do; it needn't entail much responsibility."

Mr. Wilkins had a suggestion to offer. "Leave it to me, Carter. I'm taking his form later on this morning, and I'll try him out as chief blackboard wiper or head window-opener or something of the sort."

"Thanks, Wilkins. That's a good idea."

"I should think he could cope with that without straining himself," Mr. Wilkins went on grudgingly. "It'll be his last chance, though. And if he lets us down this time . . ." He made a little grimace, shrugged, and spread out his hands with an air of helpless resignation.

"Surely," his gesture seemed to say. "Surely, even *Jennings* should be able to manage a job like chief blackboard wiper without making a mess of it!"

CHAPTER 9

THE MOBILE MAN-TRAP

A HURRYING figure, sprinting full-tilt along the corridor, caused Mr. Carter to side-step smartly as he emerged from Form 5B classroom at the beginning of morning break.

"Tut! Jennings, as usual," he said reprovingly as the athlete skidded to a halt. "How many times have I told you not to run in the corridor?"

"Sorry, sir," the boy apologised. "I'm in rather a hurry, you see. Venables has very decently agreed to lend me his skates for the whole of break."

When he remembered the feud that had been raging so bitterly at breakfast that morning, Mr. Carter found this change of heart somewhat surprising.

"Has he indeed! There are no hard feelings, then?"

"No, not any more, sir. I've forgiven him," Jennings explained graciously. "You see, Venables said he wanted to make up for getting me into trouble by making me confiscate the torch and things that I lent him in return for lending me his skates in the first place, sir."

Mr. Carter looked puzzled. "I don't quite follow."

"Oh, it's quite easy, really, sir," the boy went on in the

tones of one accustomed to dealing with slow-witted adults. "The point is that as I had to take the blame, he said I'd better take the skates as well, so we'd be quits —more or less."

"M'm!" said Mr. Carter. Baffled though he was by this queer method of reasoning, he was glad to hear that the rift had been healed. It was, he reflected, typical of those illogical schoolboy squabbles which can turn from blows to handshakes in the space of a few minutes. "Off you go then, Jennings. And no running in the corridors, remember."

The boy scuffled away, trying to hurry without actually breaking into a run. Outside on the quad he found Venables waiting for him, dangling a roller skate from each hand. It was clear from his manner that their quarrel was now a thing of the past.

"I'll just screw them up for you, and then I'll leave you to get on with it," the owner explained as he fitted the key into the adjustable toe-piece. "Temple's just had a parcel and I want to be there when he opens it, in case there's any food going." A few seconds later he rose from his stooping position and said: "There! Firm as a rock! They won't come loose now, not even if you go belting round at forty miles an hour."

He slipped the key into his pocket and ran off to attend the parcel-opening ceremony. A moment later Darbishire came trotting across the quad, attracted by the sight of his friend's flailing arms and wobbling legs.

"I haven't quite got the feel of these things yet," Jennings confided, as Darbishire extended a steadying hand. "After all, it's only the second time I've tried them. You walk round with me for a bit so I can grab hold of you if I feel myself falling. . . . Only for a couple of laps, mind," he added hurriedly. "I'll be all right when I get going."

Darbishire was inclined to be sceptical. "Huh! I knew you weren't much good at this caper, really. If you could go on one leg, for instance, or spin round like a rotating gun-turret it might be worth watching."

"Well, perhaps I could, but not on *these* skates. They're

82

different from the ones I learnt on," Jennings defended himself. "You see, mine had got straps instead of these toe-piece gadgets: they sort of put me off."

"That's a feeble excuse, if ever I heard one. You mean to tell me that . . . Hey! Look out!"

The sentence finished in a wail of protest as Jennings suddenly lost his balance and clutched Darbishire round the neck in a movement that caused both boys to lose their feet like a collapsing rugger scrum.

When they had disentangled themselves, Jennings tried again. This time his movements were better controlled, and very soon he was able to discard his human leaning-post and venture alone round the asphalt in ever widening circles.

Even so, progress was difficult for he had to exercise

great care to steer clear of the groups of boys playing with tennis balls, and others, headed by Binns and Blotwell, who were racing about madly in some sort of chasing game of their own invention.

As Jennings was completing his fifteenth lap the bell rang for the end of break. At once the improvised football matches came to an end, and the Binns commandos ceased slaughtering the Blotwell paratroopers. The quad cleared rapidly as the boys ran indoors, and by the time Jennings had made his way across to where his friend was waiting for him, everyone else had disappeared from view.

"Buck up and get the skates off, Jen. Old Wilkie's taking us for geog next lesson, and you know what he's like if we're late," Darbishire reminded him.

"All right, I won't be a sec. I can't get them off without the gadget, though."

Darbishire looked blank. "What gadget?"

"The key to unscrew them with. Venables has got it. He put them on for me." Jennings glanced round the deserted quad and a puzzled look came into his eyes. "That's funny. Where on earth has he got to?"

"Who, Venables? He's gone into class, I shouldn't wonder," Darbishire replied. "He's got enough sense not to be late for Old Wilkie's lesson."

"Yes, but . . . Oh, fish-hooks! This is frantic! How does he think I'm going to get these wretched things off if I haven't got the thing to unscrew them with!"

Darbishire was slow to grasp the gravity of the situation. "You'll have to manage without it, then. Can't you just take your feet out?"

Jennings bent down and tugged at the metal toe-piece. It was fastened firmly in position and no amount of pulling or pushing would make it yield a fraction of an inch. Furthermore, a quick glance showed that it was impossible to unscrew the toepiece by hand, for the key had to be inserted into a hollow metal tube before the thread could be engaged.

"I shall never get them off without the key. It's like being caught in a mobile man-trap," he grumbled. "Look,

Darbi, you go indoors and see if you can find Venables."

"But there isn't *time*," Darbishire protested wildly. "The bell went hours ago. Old Wilkie may be on his way up by now."

In point of fact, such a state of affairs was unlikely in theory, though quite possible in practice. According to the time-table, the lesson was not due to start until five minutes after the sounding of the bell; but it was unwise to rely on this period of grace, for it frequently happened that a master would arrive in his classroom early and expect to find his form ready and waiting.

Jennings glanced down at his feet again. The only solution was to take off his shoes and thus remove the skates at the same time. With the welt still gripped in the metal claw, he untied his shoelace and wriggled one foot free. His big toe peeped through a hole in his sock, and the pinkness of his heel was visible through a similar hole at the other end.

"Wow! Look at those massive great potatoes!" he exclaimed. "They were clean on yesterday, too."

Darbishire danced with impatience. "Never mind the potatoes, you clodpoll!" he fumed. "This is a race against time. Get the other one off, quick!"

"Yes, of course." Jennings stooped once more and fumbled with the fastening of his second shoe. This time he was not so lucky, for instead of coming undone the lace resolved itself into a tight knot.

"Tut! Now look what's happened," he complained. "That's what comes of being in a hurry: it makes you pull the wrong lace—or rather, the wrong end of the right lace."

"Well, don't just stand there making speeches about it. Try and get it undone."

But the knot was beyond the power of human fingernails to unravel. Jennings wasted a full minute before he was obliged to admit defeat, and when Darbishire tried he merely succeeded in pulling the knot tighter than before. They could not cut it, for neither of the boys had a penknife in his pocket, and the lace was so strong that it defied their efforts to break it.

Darbishire eyed the tangled lace with growing despair. "You'll just have to leave it till you get into class and find Venables."

Had it not been for the encumbrance on his right foot Jennings would have joined in Darbishire's dance of impatience. As it was he had to be content with marking time, somewhat unevenly, and waving his arms in helpless frustration.

"But I *can't* go and find Venables like this!" he cried. "I can't go stonking into class in one sock and one roller skate."

"You can if you come *now*, before Old Wilkie gets there," Darbishire urged.

"You said he'd be there already."

"Yes, I know, but—well, he sometimes gives us a few minutes after the bell. If we go right away there's still a chance we'll beat him to it, but if you're going to hang about nattering . . ."

"Come on then, quick," Jennings agreed. "You carry this other skate, and go ahead and make sure there's no one about on the stairs."

Half-scooting and half-walking, he began to make his way across the quad, the uneven length of his legs causing him to flounder with an ungainly limp. At the edge of the quad there was a gravel path to be crossed, and here his progress was impeded by the sharp-edged pebbles pricking his unprotected foot.

From the doorway Darbishire urged him on with frantic gestures of haste, and then dashed back inside to make sure that the coast was clear. His report was reassuring: the staircase was deserted, and sounds of conversation wafting into the hall from the staff room indicated that some of the masters, at any rate, had not yet dispersed to their classrooms. With luck, they might yet win their race against time.

"We'll just have to hope Old Wilkie's still in there swilling his coffee," Darbishire whispered as Jennings limped in through the side door. "If you nip up the stairs pretty quickly you can skate the rest of the way along the corridor."

Outside on the concrete the whirring of the rollers had not seemed out of place, but on the polished floorboards of the hall the noise sounded deafening. Darbishire was in an agony of suspense. The staff room was a bare ten yards away, and at any moment the door might open and a master poke his head out seeking the cause of the commotion.

"Ssh! Ssh! Don't make such a row!" he mouthed.

"I can't help it. It rattles," Jennings protested hoarsely.

By now they had reached the stairs, and though Jennings put most of his weight on his stockinged foot, the rattle and thud of the roller skate on the uncarpeted stair treads gave further cause for alarm.

Darbishire squirmed with apprehension. "You sound like a tug-boat hauling in its anchor chain," he protested. "Can't you walk on tiptoe, or something?"

"Tiptoe? On roller skates? I'd like to see you . . ."

"Well, hang on to the banisters and hop, then."

In this way Jennings reached the top of the stairs. Thenceforward his journey was easier and he was able to scoot his way along the corridor to Form 3 classroom propelling himself with his stockinged foot, while Darbishire trotted beside him and kept a guiding hand on his shoulder.

To their relief they found the classroom door was open. Obviously, Mr. Wilkins was allowing his form the full period of grace before arriving to start the lesson.

Jennings' limping entry caused a gasp of astonishment, but he was too much concerned with his plight to waste time answering the spate of questions that rained in on him from every corner of the room. Instead, he made for Venables' desk and angrily demanded his release.

"Hey, Venables, where's the key to these wretched things? You went off and left me locked in."

"Oh, sorry," Venables apologised, fumbling in his pocket. "Yes, I've got it here in my . . ." He paused, and brought forth five dirty handkerchiefs, a yard of elastic, a bundle of toffee papers, a Belgian franc and a quantity of grey fluff which he laid on the lid of his desk. "Oh, fish-hooks! I remember now; I left it downstairs in the tuck-box room."

Jennings was aghast at this further setback. "You addle-pated clodpoll. Go and get it at once, then."

To Venables this seemed unreasonable. "I can't go now. I haven't got time," he argued. "Old Wilkie will be here in a . . ."

"He's coming up the stairs now," announced Atkinson who was keeping a lookout by the door.

"This is frantic!" wailed Jennings. "What am I going to do?"

"Go and sit down. He won't notice anything if you keep your feet under the desk and don't fidget about," Venables advised.

"Yes, but . . ."

"I'll get it for you after school. You'll be all right, honestly."

Heavy footsteps approaching the open door of the classroom warned Jennings that there was not a moment to be lost. Bobbing up and down like a marker buoy in a rough sea, he hopped and scooted across the room to his back-row desk by the window. Behind him scuttled Darbishire, who reached the safety of the adjoining desk only to find that he was still clutching the other skate firmly attached to Jennings' left shoe. Unable to think what to do with it, he waved the object helplessly in the air and then, with sudden inspiration, dropped it in the waste-paper basket in the corner behind the desks.

At the same moment Mr. Wilkins marched briskly in through the door to begin the lesson. Having allowed his class the full five minutes grace, he was anxious to proceed with the morning's work without further loss of time.

"Right! Now first we're going to draw a map showing the rainfall of Australia," he boomed as he sat down at the master's desk. "Open your atlases at page 57."

"Please, sir, I haven't got a pen," complained Martin-Jones.

"You won't need a pen," Mr. Wilkins replied. "You'll need pencils, india-rubbers, and . . ." His last words started a train of thought in his mind: ever since his ill-fated book inspection, the mention of india-rubber caused him to think of Jennings. And thinking of Jennings reminded him of the offer he had made to Mr. Carter after breakfast that morning. He could deal with the matter in a few moments while the boys were thumbing through their atlases. . . . So he thought!

"Ah, yes, let me see, now; where's Jennings?" Mr. Wilkins went on in crisp, though kindly, tones.

"Here, sir," said a voice by the window.

"Well, listen to me. I've had a word with some of the other masters about your conduct in the dormitory last night."

Form 3 stopped fidgeting and listened with attention. Here was a subject more to their liking than the distribution of rainfall in Australia.

"Mr. Carter thinks that there may have been some—er —mitigating circumstances."

Jennings looked blank. "May have been *what*, sir?"

"He thinks that perhaps you were not entirely to blame," Mr. Wilkins translated. "So with the Head's approval we have decided to give you one last chance."

"Thank you, sir," said Jennings politely. If he sat quite still and kept his feet together he should be safe enough for the rest of the lesson, he told himself.

"One last chance," Mr. Wilkins repeated with emphasis. "A final opportunity for you to make good. And that being the case I'm going to try you out as—er—I'm going to create a new post of official classroom tidier. It will be up to you to see that the inkwells are filled, that there's no waste paper on the floor, and that the blackboard is clean and ready for use whenever a master comes in to take a lesson."

"Yes, sir."

"And I shall expect you to carry out your duties in an intelligent and responsible fashion."

"I'll try, sir," said Jennings. He was pleased with his new appointment. Come what may, he would see that his form master's confidence in him was not misplaced.

"Right!" Mr. Wilkins glanced at the blackboard and noticed that it was covered with lists of French verbs which the form had been studying in the last lesson before break. "You can start right away, then. Come up and clean the board for me."

Jennings stiffened. The blackboard swam before his eyes and he clutched the lid of his desk in apprehension.

"*Me*, sir?" he faltered. "Go and do it *now*, sir? Straight away this minute, do you mean?"

"Of course I mean straight away," Mr. Wilkins retorted. "I want to use it. There's no point in cleaning the board this afternoon when I want to draw a map of Australia this morning, is there?"

"No, sir. Only I . . ." Jennings gulped and swallowed hard. There must be some excuse he could make to avoid exposing his feet! But for the life of him he was unable to think of any way of saving the situation. ". . . Well, sir, it's just that I didn't really want to leave my desk, just at the moment, sir," he finished up.

Mr. Wilkins stared at the official classroom tidier in amazement. "What on earth are you talking about, you silly little boy?" he demanded. "Here I am giving you a last chance to make up for your stupid behaviour, and you sit there making absurd excuses!" In a burst of exasperation he barked out: "Don't be ridiculous, boy. Come up here at once when I tell you to!"

Slowly, Jennings rose from his seat and limped his way along the gangway between the desks to the open space at the front of the room. It was impossible now to conceal his oddly-shod feet. The *rattle-clank* of the skate on the floorboards followed by the soft padding of his stockinged foot announced only too clearly that the newly-appointed chief blackboard wiper was reporting for duty in somewhat unusual footwear.

The effect upon Mr. Wilkins was dramatic. He shot from the master's desk like a rocket from its launching base. His eyes opened wide, his head jerked forward and his jaw dropped through an angle of thirty degrees.

"I—I—I . . . What—what—what on earth have you got on your foot, boy!"

Jennings glanced down at his feet as though only now becoming aware that there was anything odd about them.

90

"This, sir?" he queried. "This is just a—it's only a skate, sir."

"Only a *skate!*" echoed Mr. Wilkins, his voice rising to a squeak of indignation. "Roller-skating in the classroom in the middle of a geography lesson!"

"No, not really, sir. You see, Venables went off with the key, sir, and my shoelace got a knot in it and——"

"I—I—*Corwumph!* I've never in my life encountered such a fantastic exhibition of—of—of . . ." The words spluttered to a halt of speechless incredulity. Jennings, again! Jennings, as usual! It always *was* Jennings who upset the smooth running of school routine in this infuriating fashion. With an effort, Mr. Wilkins regained the power of speech. "And look at your other foot!" he stormed. "Just look at it!"

Jennings looked at it.

"Where's your shoe, boy? Where's your shoe?"

On this point Jennings was vague, and the information was kindly supplied by Darbishire.

"Please, sir, it's in the wastepaper basket," he said.

Through clenched teeth Mr. Wilkins made a noise like a vacuum brake. When he had run out of compressed air, Jennings said: "I'm sorry about the holes in my sock, sir, but they were . . ."

"*Doh!* This is too much," Mr. Wilkins thumped the master's desk in exasperation. "I choose you for a post of responsibility and you report for duty on one roller skate, two holes in your sock and your shoe thrown away in the rubbish bin! . . . It's preposterous! You're not fit to be put in charge of keeping the classroom tidy. You're not even fit to be put in charge of a piece of blotting-paper!" With mounting indignation he recalled a few of the recent disasters for which Jennings had been responsible.

"Just look at your behaviour this term. Poisonous fumes! Flaming rubbers! Tin-can window tapping! Bogus burglars! Snorkel-breathing under the blankets! And as if that wasn't enough, you come roller-skating into my class looking like a—like a . . ."

Mr. Wilkins shot a quick glance at Jennings to see what

91

he *did* look like. . . . And abruptly his tirade ceased; for the pathetic figure in the ridiculous footwear was looking such a picture of woe that Mr. Wilkins decided that he had already said enough. The boy had gone very pale, his eyes were moist and he was biting his quivering lower lip in an effort to stem the flood of misery which seemed about to overwhelm him at any moment.

In spite of his brusque manner and uncertain temper, Mr. Wilkins had a kind-hearted streak in his nature which shrank from the sight of a fellow human being in genuine distress. And there was no doubt that John Christopher Timothy Jennings was at that moment suffering very acutely indeed: so acutely, in fact, that Mr. Wilkins decided not to prolong the agony still further.

There was a short silence. Then the form master shook his head sadly and said: "You really are a silly little boy, Jennings."

The boy nodded. He could not trust himself to speak.

"I suppose that some time in the dim and distant future," Mr. Wilkins went on, echoing a sentiment which Mr. Carter had often expressed, "I suppose that eventually the day will come when you'll learn to behave like a civilised member of the community?"

This time a faint mumble of agreement accompanied the nod of the head. "I hope so, sir."

Mr. Wilkins forced a wan smile as he motioned the boy back to his seat. "That will be the day, Jennings," he said. "*That* will be the day!"

CHAPTER 10

THE ASSISTANT MASTERPIECE

By the time Venables had retrieved his key from the tuck-box room and Jennings was once more shod in conventional footwear, the geography lesson was nearly half over.

"You'll be sorry you've wasted all this time," Mr. Wilkins told the class. "I was going to allow you the last few minutes of this lesson to revise for next week's test, but there won't be time for that now—thanks to Jennings."

"*Test*, sir?" Temple inquired in aggrieved tones. "What test, sir?"

"The test that I shall be giving you next week on Australia and New Zealand," Mr. Wilkins went on, ignoring the stifled groans that his announcement caused in some parts of the room. "If you take my advice you'll do some revision in your own time, because anyone whose work isn't up to standard will be—will be . . ." Unable on the spur of the moment to think of a suitable punishment, he spread his hands in a gesture implying spine-chilling consequences. "Well, I'm warning you," he finished up.

Jennings decided to heed the warning. That evening in the half-hour before bed time he settled down to read the notes he had taken during the term. But after ten minutes of studying the climatic conditions of Australia his mind began to wander away to the more practical side of life in the southern hemisphere.

"I wouldn't mind living in Australia, Darbi," he remarked to his friend who was seated on the other side of the common-room table chewing a pencil and frowning at a sheet of paper lying before him. "I mean, you'd be able to play cricket when everyone else was playing football, wouldn't you."

Darbishire glanced up. "There'd be a bit of a hoohah on the pitch if you did that," he observed. "You might get the balls mixed up and . . ."

"No, you coot. Not on the same pitch at the same time. I mean our winter is their summer. So you could do things like, for instance, eating your Christmas dinner out in the garden if you wanted to."

"Wouldn't suit me," said Darbishire firmly. "I like snow and holly and robins and things on my Christmas cards—not a lot of weedy ice cream cornets." By way of proof he passed the sheet of paper across the table, revealing a half-finished drawing of a Yuletide scene. "There's not an awful lot of shopping days left before Christmas," he said, "so I thought I'd get cracking with a few homemade cards."

The custom of making Christmas cards towards the end of the autumn term was—like conkers—a seasonal hobby which invariably became a popular craze as the end of term drew near. Darbishire, however, believed in starting early, for it was now only the last week in November and the term had still three weeks to run.

His first card, which he proposed sending to his godmother, depicted a group of people with completely round heads, fingers shaped like bunches of bananas, and rickety legs with feet splayed out at right angles. Each character in the group wore what looked like an ill-fitting bowler hat which, instead of sitting snugly on his circular cranium, merely touched the circumference at one point like a tangent to a circle. The wearing of this headgear must have been a balancing feat of no mean order, especially as the characters appeared to be standing on an iceberg with a gradient of one in three.

According to Darbishire, the scene represented carol singers in the snow, and this was borne out by phrases from well-known carols ballooning out from the mouths of the singers in block letters of red crayon.

Jennings was critical of his friend's prowess as an artist. "A pretty feeble effort if you ask me," he said. "All these titchy little people with skinny legs! And anyway, why don't they eat their christmas puddings instead of carrying them about on their heads?"

"Those are their hats, you grisly specimen," Darbishire defended himself. "You wait till I've coloured it, and then you'll see. I'm going to do lots of cards from now on. It makes the end of term seem a lot nearer if you start doing Christmassy things in good time."

On this point Jennings was in full agreement. "Why stop at Christmas cards, then?" he demanded. Would it not be even better if they were to make some decorations to hang up in the common room in honour of the Christmas party which was always held on the last day of term?

"It'd be a super thing to do," he went on with rising enthusiasm as the idea took shape in his mind. "We could make Chinese lanterns and miles and miles of paper chains and things."

Darbishire's eyes shone with delight. "Yes, rather. We've got about twenty days before the end of term party; so if we each made, say, a yard of paper chain every day that'd give us twenty yards—forty yards between the two of us."

"That's nothing," Jennings retorted. "When this craze takes on everyone'll want to join in. Let's see, now. Say seventy-nine chaps all working like beavers to make a yard a day. . . ."

"I wouldn't count on everyone," Darbishire said cautiously. "Say fifty; it's easier to work out the quantities."

"All right, then, fifty. Fifty chaps making twenty yards equals—um—ah—Wow! A thousand yards! "

They gaped at each other in awe as their minds conjured up a picture of the common room festooned with more than half a mile of coloured paper chains. The imagination boggled at the sheer length of the undertaking. Why, laid out in a line the chain would stretch from the school to Linbury village; fashioned into the tail of a kite it would rise to the height of a mountain top before the last link had even left the ground!

It was Darbishire who raised the first practical objection. "Yes, but where on earth should we get all that paper from?" he asked.

Jennings dismissed the difficulty with a wave of his hand. "We'll go through all the wastepaper baskets and use wrapping paper from chaps' parcels and stuff," he said airly. "And if that isn't enough we'll . . ." He glanced round seeking inspiration and his eye fell upon the geography notebook which he had just been studying. "Well, what about old exercise books?"

Darbishire pursed his lips in doubt. "There might be a bit of a hoo-hah if we did that," he said.

"I don't see why. Not if they're used up and finished with, that is."

"I know, but all the same . . ."

"Take this old geog book, for instance," Jennings went on, waving the green-covered object under Darbishire's nose. "I finished it up this afternoon, and I shall be going on to my new one next lesson. Okay, then. Why not use this for scrap? Only in an emergency, of course, if we run short of paper."

This answer seemed reasonably convincing. After all, a number of old exercise books were often thrown away at the end of term when the desks were being tidied. But this was only done, Darbishire recalled, when it was obvious that the owners had no further use for them. "Have it your own way then," he conceded as the dormitory bell put an end to further discussion. "Only don't blame me if the Archbeako or someone kicks up a fuss."

Needless to say, the "Jennings' Plan" of interior decoration was acclaimed with enthusiasm by most of the younger boarders when the details were explained to them. A few alterations were agreed upon; for example, it was felt that half a mile of paper chain in the common room was an excessive amount, and instead it was decided to spread the decorations over a larger area. Binns and Blotwell devised a scheme to turn Form 1 classroom into a fairy grotto; and a competition was arranged to see which dormitory could produce the most artistic results.

As a precaution, permission was sought from Mr. Carter who said he had no objections to offer provided that only waste paper was used and that the boys did not begin to hang up their decorations until the day of the party. "We don't want the school looking like a corporation salvage dump before it's absolutely necessary," he observed.

In the days that followed, the rustle of ever-lengthening paper chains could be heard in most parts of the building. The process of manufacture was simple: paper was cut into strips, coloured with crayon, and the ends gummed together to form a link round the adjoining strip.

Soon most of the available waste paper had been used up and the boys were obliged to seek for materials elsewhere. Writing-pads, magazines and letters from home were pressed into service; although at this early stage of the proceedings nobody ventured to use old exercise books. They took care, too, to heed Mr. Carter's instructions about keeping their handiwork stored away in lockers and cupboards, for any odd lengths of chain left lying about were invariably swept up by Robinson, the odd job man, and consigned to dustbin or bonfire.

As the work went on it encouraged a feeling that the spirit of Christmas was in the air—or at any rate, just round the corner; and this meant that any time that could be spared from the decorations was spent in the annual pastime of making seasonal greeting cards.

Atkinson was painting a Christmas card for a favourite uncle when Jennings entered Form 3 classroom shortly before Mr. Wilkins' geography lesson on Friday afternoon.

"That's a weedy-looking horse and cart you've got there," he criticised, peering over the artist's shoulder. "Why haven't you drawn any wheels?"

"It isn't a horse and cart; it's a reindeer pulling a sledge. Can't you see its antlers?" Atkinson retorted curtly.

"Oh, is that what they are? I thought it was a television aerial sprouting out of that pillar box just behind it."

Atkinson scowled at the critic in disapproval. "I'd have you know, Jennings," he said with dignity, "that what you call a pillar box happens to be Father Christmas. The trouble with you is that you don't know the first thing about Art."

"Well, I bet I could draw a better-looking character than that! "

"I bet you couldn't!" said Atkinson derisively. "Go ahead and prove it if you're so clever. I challenge you! Do your best drawing of a man and we'll get someone to say if it's as good as my Father Christmas."

Stung by this reflection on his prowess, Jennings opened his desk and began rummaging for pencil and paper. "All right, then," he agreed. "Just wait till I find something to draw on, and I'll show you!"

Apart from some brown paper which he was intending

to use for the decorations, Jennings could find nothing suitable on which to demonstrate his skill as an artist. Impatiently he lifted out a pile of exercise books, chose one at random and opened it at a clean page.

"Hey, you can't draw in that, Jen—not in your geography book," Atkinson warned him.

"I can easily rub it out again," Jennings replied airily. "I won't press too hard."

Lightly he skimmed over the surface of the page, sketching the head and shoulders of a middle-aged man. As a work of art the drawing was far from perfect: the ears were too large, the nose out of alignment, the eyes were like marbles and the neck showed the subject to be suffering from a severe attack of mumps.

But to Darbishire, who had just strolled up to see what was going on, the drawing seemed to bear some resemblance to a figure he knew well. With marked interest he said: "I say, Jen, that's jolly good. It couldn't be more like him if you'd copied it from life."

Jennings looked up puzzled. It was just a lightning sketch of a man's head, so far as he was aware. "Like who?" he asked.

"It's obvious who it's meant to be," Darbishire went on, gurgling with suppressed laughter. He called to a small group of boys who had just come into the room in readiness for afternoon school. "Hey, Venables! Temple! Come over here and have a look at old Jen's drawing. It's lobsterous!"

Mildly curious, they gathered round the artist, leaning on his shoulders and breathing heavily down the back of his neck.

"Who does it remind you of?" Darbishire demanded.

Like Jennings, Temple and Venables could see no resemblance to any living person. "The abominable snowman?" Temple hazarded.

"Gosh, no! Try again."

"Well, just an *ordinary* snowman, then?"

Darbishire tut-tutted like a turnstile. He was amazed that anyone could be so dense.

"I'd say it was Old Wilkie," said Temple.

"No, no, no! Stand farther back—the farther the better, really." . . . *Now* can you see?"

Temple made a wild guess. One name seemed as good as another to him. "He looks a bit ossified to me. I'd say it was Old Wilkie."

Darbishire beamed his congratulations. "Of course! Who else? It's just like him, isn't it?"

In point of fact the likeness to Mr. Wilkins was wholly imaginary. Nevertheless, Darbishire's enthusiasm swayed the judgment of his audience who were only too ready to agree with his opinion. Each of them felt that it was better that the picture *should* look like Mr. Wilkins than that it shouldn't! Temple, for example, was delighted with his brilliant powers of perception in guessing the truth so quickly: Venables was anxious to keep in Darbishire's good books, as it was rumoured that he was expecting a parcel from his godmother: Atkinson did not like Mr. Wilkins and was quite willing to see him caricatured: while Jennings was reluctant to lose his reputation as a cartoonist of exceptional skill. Thus, by pooling their powers of imagination and wishful thinking the group were convinced that the likeness was genuine.

"Yes, so it is. I can see it now," said Venables. He laughed, somewhat more loudly than necessary, to show his appreciation.

"Fancy us not spotting it before," said Atkinson, his argument with Jennings now forgotten. "It's an absolute masterpiece, if you ask me."

The cartoonist breathed on his fingernails and polished them on his pullover to show that such feats of draughtsmanship came easily to the skilled pencil of J. C. T. Jennings.

"I wouldn't go so far as to say that," he said with becoming modesty. "Still, as it's a drawing of Sir you *could* call it an assistant masterpiece, couldn't you!"

The group broke into convulsions of merriment at what they seemed to think was the wittiest retort they had heard for a long time. They sagged at the knees in helpless hilarity and explained the joke to one another over and over again in case anyone had been slow to grasp its point.

Encouraged by the response of his audience, Jennings decided to strengthen the so-called resemblance of his sketch still further. He would make it appear to be saying one of Mr. Wilkins' favourite expressions. Frowning with concentration he drew a balloon coming out of the lop-sided mouth and inserted the words, *Doh! You silly little boy!*

The bell for afternoon school sounded as he was add-ing the finishing touches, and as the rest of Form 3 straggled in, singly and in groups, Darbishire was quick to call their attention to the assistant masterpiece.

"I say, come and look at this," he sang out to Rum-below and Martin-Jones as they passed Jennings' desk. "Can you guess who it's supposed to be?"

Martin-Jones grinned his appreciation as he glanced down at the exercise book. By itself the sketch would have meant nothing to him, but the caption provided the obvious answer. "Yes, of course. It's Old Wilkie."

"There you are, you see," Darbishire cried in triumph. "If Martin-Jones recognises it, anyone would!"

Jennings was delighted. It seemed that he was a better artist than he had thought. Just to be on the safe side, however, he added a title to his work. *L. P. Wilkins, Esq.,* he wrote underneath in sprawling capitals.

At that moment the original of the lightning sketch arrived to begin the lesson. Hurriedly Jennings turned over the page. On no account must Mr. Wilkins be allowed to catch sight of his unflattering portrait.

The geography test occupied most of the lesson. Jen-nings was thankful that he had done a certain amount of revision in his own time, for he found that he could an-swer most of the questions reasonably well. Indeed, he finished the test with ten minutes to spare.

This was all to the good, for it meant that he could now devote the rest of the time to a problem that de-manded his immediate attention—the question of what to do about the assistant masterpiece. Obviously, if Mr. Wilkins was not to see his portrait, it must be rubbed out or removed before the book was collected at the end of the lesson.

At the same time, it would be a pity to destroy the drawing while there was still a number of art-lovers who had not yet had a chance of seeing it, Jennings reflected. Surely, a work of such merit should be preserved for posterity. He was sorry, now, that he had chosen his geography book for the purpose. But how could he have known in advance that his portrait would be acclaimed such a success? Perhaps if he was careful he could cut the page out without being seen.

He glanced at the master's desk. Mr. Wilkins was immersed in an atlas. Now was the time!

Jennings slipped the book into his desk, leaving the lid raised as a cover for his operations. Should Mr. Wilkins chance to look up from his reading he might well think that his pupil was getting his books ready for the next lesson. From a cardboard box in his desk, Jennings extracted his penknife and opened the blade. Then he folded the tell-tale page along the margin and inserted the blade in its fold.

"Jennings!"

Mr. Wilkins' voice rang out so suddenly that the boy jumped as though he had been stung.

"What are you doing inside that desk?"

Jennings' face was a picture of guilty confusion as he hastily shut the exercise book and pushed it towards the back of his desk.

"I—er—I wasn't really doing anything, sir. Nothing much, that is," he faltered.

"Don't prevaricate, boy. And don't talk to me over the top of a desk!"

Obediently, Jennings closed the lid.

"Now then, what's that penknife doing in your hand?"

"This knife, sir? Well, you see, I'd finished the test and I was just filling in time—er—cutting a piece of paper, sir."

Mr. Wilkins' mind leaped at once to the wrong conclusion. "Cutting up paper, eh! These Christmas decorations are getting completely out of hand!" he barked.

"It's bad enough with you boys spending all your *free* time on these everlasting contraptions, and I'm certainly not going to have you doing it in class, whether you've finished your work or not."

"No, sir."

"Bring that penknife to me. I shall confiscate it."

With a slow tread Jennings approached the master's desk and placed the penknife in Mr. Wilkins' outstretched hand. "Shall I be able to have it back at the end of term, sir?" he inquired anxiously.

"That's for me to decide," came the curt answer.

"But, sir . . . "

"Don't argue with me. You've caused quite enough distraction already when other boys are still working," Mr. Wilkins said. "And that being so you can leave the room and stay out for the rest of the lesson."

Outside in the corridor Jennings reviewed his fortunes. It was bad luck about the penknife, he told himself; he might get it back before the holidays—and then again he might not. You never quite knew with Mr. Wilkins. The only thing you could do was to be decent to the man for a week or so and hope he'd be in a good mood when you asked him to return your property.

Apart from losing his penknife, though, things hadn't gone too badly, thanks to Mr. Wilkins jumping to the wrong conclusion. There was no danger now of the drawing falling into his hands, for as soon as the lesson was over he could go back into the classroom and remove the evidence to a place of safety before . . .

Jennings' train of thought was broken by the bell sounding for the end of the lesson, and a moment later Mr. Wilkins emerged from the classroom. The boy stood aside to let him pass, and as he did so he caught sight of the pile of exercise books tucked under Mr. Wilkins' arm.

A sudden terrifying suspicion flashed into Jennings' mind and his hand shot up to his mouth in alarm. Supposing, just supposing . . .

In a state of wild panic he dashed into the classroom and collided with Bromwich (now fully restored to health) who was making for the door.

"Hey, Bromo, quick! Who collected up the books after the test?" he demanded.

"I did. Sir told me to," Bromwich replied. "You needn't worry about *your* book, though—it's safe enough."

"Phew! Thank goodness for that," Jennings gasped with relief. "I felt sure I hadn't left it out, but I was a bit worried in case . . . "

"You needn't have worried," Bromwich assured him. "When I saw it wasn't on top of your desk I rummaged about inside till I found it."

"What!" Jennings stared at the book collector in wide-eyed dismay. "You—you mean you actually took my book out of my desk and gave it to Old Wilkie?"

"Well, of course I did," said Bromwich. "You want to have your test marked, don't you?"

CHAPTER 11

AUTOGRAPH HUNT

THE full horror of his plight swept over Jennings like a tidal wave. He flapped his fingers in frustration and marked time on the floorboards like a honey bee drumming out a message to his fellow workers on the threshold of the hive.

"You great big addle-pated clodpoll, Bromo!" he stormed as the dance of the bees worked up to a frenzied finale. "What on earth did you want to go and do a thing like that for!"

Bromwich stared at him in bewilderment. "I don't know what you're woffling about," he protested. "No harm in getting your book out of your desk, was there?"

"No harm!" Jennings echoed bitterly. "Oh, no! No harm at all! It only so happens that you've given Sir a comic drawing of himself, with his name underneath in large letters. He'll go through the roof like an H-bomb when he sees it."

Bromwich emitted a little whistle of sympathy. "Phew! Super sorrow," he apologised. "Still, you can't blame me for it. How was I to know what you'd done?"

"Everybody knew," Jennings protested wildly. "Pretty well the whole form saw it before the lesson started."

But Bromwich, it appeared, was an exception; and though he deplored the accident he felt that it was hardly his responsibility. He had acted in good faith, he pointed out, and if Jennings insisted upon drawing unflattering cartoons of members of the staff it was surely up to him to see that they did not fall into the wrong hands.

There was no time, then, to discuss the matter further, for at that moment Mr. Carter arrived to take an English lesson; and all through the two remaining periods Jennings had to sit and chafe in silent frustration. One thought was uppermost in his mind: somehow or other, by hook or by crook, the tell-tale evidence *must* be retrieved befor the books were corrected.

With this intention he hurried along to the staff room as soon as the class was dismissed at the end of afternoon school. He found Mr. Wilkins seated in an armchair, poring over a crossword puzzle. On the table beside him were Form 3's geography books, neatly stacked and, as yet, unopened.

"Sir, please, sir, may I have my geography book back for a minute, sir?" Jennings asked.

Mr. Wilkins did not bother to look up from his crossword. "Of course you can't have it back—not until I've finished marking it," he replied, his mind busy with clue number 23 *across*.

"But, sir, it's terribly important. I've just remembered something."

A flicker of resentment passed across Mr. Wilkins' features. He had been on the point of solving number 23 *across*, and the interruption had broken the thread of his concentration.

"You know perfectly well you can't make alterations when the test is over," he said severely. "For all I know you may have looked up the right answers and . . ."

"Oh, no, it's nothing like that!" Jennings interposed.

"I don't want to alter anything I've written in the test, sir."

"Then why do you want your book back?"

"Well, sir, I—er—I . . ." the words tailed away. There was no short answer to this question, and to persist with his plea would raise suspicions in Mr. Wilkins' mind. Awkwardly Jennings mumbled: "I just thought I'd like to have it, sir. Not for anything very special, really."

The flicker of resentment turned to a look of bewilderment. "I haven't the faintest idea what you're talking about. You'll get your book back to-morrow when I've marked the test, and not before." Mr. Wilkins pointed to the door with the stem of his pipe. "Out!" he commanded.

In chastened mood, Jennings returned to his classroom where he found three of his friends searching through the wastepaper basket for raw materials with which to construct further lengths of paper chain.

"Something terrible's happened," he announced from the doorway. In a voice of gloom he outlined the facts of the latest disaster.

It came as a shock to Darbishire, Temple and Atkinson to hear that the portrait had gone astray.

"Wow! and his name underneath in big letters, too!" breathed Darbishire in horror. "What on earth are you going to do?"

"It's a pity you made it such a *comic* drawing," said Atkinson, shaking his head sadly. "After all, his ears don't *really* stick out like aeroplane wings, do they?"

"And you needn't have made his nose quite so lopsided, either," Temple pointed out.

"Or drawn his eyes popping out like organ stops," Darbishire added. "And all that guff about 'you silly little boy' that he was woffling into the balloon. I can just imagine what he'll say when he sees it."

"He mustn't see it—ever!" Jennings cried wildly. "I must get hold of the book and rub it out while there's still time."

The decision, though admirable in theory, was fraught with certain hazards when considered from a practical

106

point of view. To begin with, nobody could tell for certain when Mr. Wilkins would begin marking the test. Furthermore, the task of erasing the drawing could be done only when the staff room was empty and the masters were engaged in other parts of the building. But Jennings was not deterred by the difficulties. Time was short; the situation was desperate. Whatever the risk involved, he must do something.

"I shall go back to the staff room directly after tea with a piece of india-rubber and knock on the door," he announced.

Darbishire pursed his lips doubtfully. "I should use your knuckles. No one will ever hear you tapping with a bit of bungee."

Jennings rounded on his friend warmly. "Don't be so stark raving haywire, Darbi! The bungee is only for rubbing out the drawing if there aren't any masters there."

"Yes, but supposing there are?"

"In that case I shall—I shall . . ." Jennings racked his brains for some reasonable excuse. "I shall just say something like—er—do they think it'll be fine for the match to-morrow. And then I'll go back and have another shot later."

The plan was received with grimaces of disapproval.

"Too chancy," was Atkinson's verdict. "They might still be there when you went back, and you couldn't keep on all evening popping in every five minutes to ask them about the weather. They'd smell a rat."

"Well, you think of something better, then," Jennings urged. "All of you! Don't just stand there like a lot of spare dinners. All think of something!"

They thought! . . . And for some minutes there was an atmosphere of quiet concentration as the little group wrestled with the problem before them. It was Jennings, as usual, who was to blame for the trouble, but they were willing—within reasonable limits—to do what they could to help him out of it.

After some discussion it was agreed that Jennings' chances of success would be increased if he had a secret band of helpers all working to achieve the same result.

107

It might well be that the first boy to present himself at the staff room would find the room occupied, and having made his excuse would then have to retire. The second person might share the same fate if luck was against him; and even possibly the third. But with *four* boys all timing their visits and varying their excuses, surely *one* would be bound to succeed.

Upon reflection they decided it was unlikely that Mr. Wilkins would begin marking the tests until the boys were in bed, for it was known that he was on duty that evening. The best time for the operation would be during the half-hour before the dormitory bell, when the master on duty might well be occupied making his routine tour of the building.

"That's what we'll do, then," Jennings decided when the plan had been thoroughly discussed. "We'll synchronise our watches so we don't all get there at the same time, and we'll draw names out of a hat to see who goes first."

"Wow! How super!" The conspirators' eyes sparkled with excitement. Synchronised watches, split-second timing and the drawing of lots raised the whole project to the level of a secret commando raid. Here was an adventure calling for stout hearts and nerves of steel.

Accordingly, they wrote their names on scraps of paper and shuffled them in a pencil-box. The atmosphere was tense as Jennings drew lots to determine the order of attack.

"We'll go at five-minute intervals," he announced when the ballot was completed. "The first chap knocks on the door at 19.35 hours precisely."

"What time's that?" queried Atkinson.

"Twenty-five to eight, of course. If the staff room's empty he rubs out the drawing and reports to the others that the job's been done. If there's anyone there, of course, he just makes his excuse and goes away, and the next chap has a bash five minutes later."

Darbishire wrinkled his nose and said: "I can never think of a decent excuse when I want one."

"You'd better start thinking one up right away, then,"

Jennings replied. "Pretty well anything will do, really. For instance, one of us could ask him to sign their autograph book . . ."

"Good scheme!" the conspirators approved, each making a mental note of this fool-proof pretext.

". . . and somebody else could ask him—er—er . . ." For the moment he was unable to think of a suitable alternative. "Well, somebody else could ask him something else; it doesn't matter what. The main thing is that we all four go at different times and all have different excuses."

The tea bell rang as Jennings finished speaking. The meeting broke up and the boys trotted downstairs to the dining hall well-satisfied with the preparations they had made. And indeed, so far as the accurate timing of their visits was concerned, the plan was destined to work well. It was, therefore a pity that they had not a proper chance to discuss in detail the excuses which they might be called upon to offer. For this proved to be the weak link in an otherwise flawless scheme.

At half-past seven that evening Mr. Wilkins laid aside his unfinished crossword puzzle and rose to his feet. "Duty calls," he remarked to Mr. Hind who was the only other occupant of the staff room. "It's time I took a stroll round to see what those boys are getting up to."

Mr. Hind removed his curly pipe from his mouth and polished the bowl on the side of his nose—a habit of his which, he claimed, gave the pipe its rich and lustrous shine.

"I suppose you wouldn't care to change duties with me, would you?" he said. "I've been asked to go to the cinema to-morrow night when I should be on duty, and I'm looking for someone to take over for me."

Mr. Wilkins nodded. "Suits me—if you'll do this evening instead. It'll give me a chance to get on with marking Form 3's geography test. The Head's waiting for the monthly orders, so the sooner I get it finished the better."

Mr. Wilkins sat down again as his colleague left the room to begin his tour of supervision duty. Form 3 geography test! Yes, of course. He would start marking the books straight away, he decided. And then the unfinished crossword puzzle caught his eye. . . . Perhaps he could allow himself just a few minutes of relaxation before he began.

Clue number 17 *down* offered a most intriguing challenge, calling for his immediate attention: and then there was that anagram in clue number 31 *across*. Keenly interested though he was in Form 3's progress in geography, there were times, Mr. Wilkins felt, when even the most devoted schoolmaster might allow himself a brief respite from his labours. He picked up the crossword puzzle and frowned thoughtfully at clue number 17 *down*.

At twenty-five to eight there was a tap on the staff room door. "Come in!" called Mr. Wilkins.

The visitor was Temple. He gulped slightly at seeing the armchair occupied, and then fumbled in his pocket for an autograph album.

"Please, sir, would you write something in my book, please, sir?" he asked.

Mr. Wilkins nodded. The request was not unusual. "You just want my signature, I take it?"

"Yes, sir. Of course, you can write something else as well, if you like, sir," Temple suggested. "Something like, say, for instance, *By hook or by crook I'll be first in your book*, sir."

"All right. Leave the book here. I'll do it later."

Temple trotted out of the room shaking his head in disappointment. It was too bad Old Wilkie being there. Still, he'd done his best and now it was up to the others!

At seven-forty Mr. Wilkins' train of thought was again interrupted by a knock on the door. This time the caller was Darbishire. He looked ill at ease and stood half in and half out of the door twiddling an india-rubber between his fingers.

"What is it, Darbishire? Do you want to see me?"

"Er—no, sir, not really. That is, I didn't think you'd be here, sir," came the faltering reply.

Mr. Wilkins frowned. "My dear boy, if you don't want to see me and you thought I wasn't here, what did you knock at the door for?"

110

With an effort Darbishire pulled himself together. "I just wondered whether you'd—er—whether you'd very kindly write something in my autograph book," he said, struggling to produce the album from his trouser pocket.

Mr. Wilkins was surprised. One request was natural enough, but two on one evening seemed to be carrying things to extremes.

"Just anything will do, sir," Darbishire twittered nervously. "Like, say, for instance, *By hook or by crook I'll be first in your book*, or something like that."

"I'm rather busy at the moment," Mr. Wilkins replied. "However anxious I am to be first in your book it will have to wait until I've finished doing my—er—until I've finished marking your geography books."

The words caused Darbishire to jump like a startled faun. "Our geography books! Oh, golly! You haven't corrected them yet, then, sir?"

"No, Darbishire, I haven't. And if any more people come knocking at the door and interrupting me, it's extremely unlikely that I shall get them done this evening, at all."

The implied rebuke had a reassuring effect upon Darbishire. "Oh, good-o, sir. I mean—er—well, I'd better be going now." So saying, he dropped his album on the staff room table and fled.

Five minutes passed during which time Mr. Wilkins solved the puzzling anagram and then went on to consider clue number 29 *across*.

Then Atkinson arrived. Like Darbishire, he seemed vague about the purpose of his visit.

"Oh, there you are, sir! I thought perhaps there wasn't anybody in here," he said, as though in explanation. "Or rather, I mean, I thought you were on duty this evening."

"Oh, did you!" Mr. Wilkins said with deep suspicion. "And so you decided you'd stroll into the staff room to see what it looked like when it was empty, I suppose."

"Oh, no, sir. I remember now, I *do* want to see you rather urgently as it happens, sir." The boy fumbled in his pocket and brought out an autograph album. "I was wondering whether you'd mind writing something in this for me, sir? It needn't be anything very much. Just something like, *By hook or by crook I'll be first in your book,* sir. And then if you'll sign . . ." The words tailed away as he looked up and caught sight of Mr. Wilkins' expression.

"What game are you silly little boys playing?" the master demanded angrily. By now he felt sure that the queue of callers were engaged in some sort of attempt to be funny at his expense. "You all come parading into the staff room to find me and then tell me it's the one place where you don't expect me to be."

"No, sir, it's not like that really."

"And all this business about signing autograph books," Mr. Wilkins continued on a rising note. "Considering the rush there's been this evening, anyone would think I was the star performer of a television quiz programme! "

Atkinson looked down at his shoes and said nothing. It was hardly fair of Old Wilkie to put all the blame on him like this. After all, the whole thing was Jennings' fault really. And what was all this about *previous* demands for autographs? So far as Atkinson was aware, his was the first request of its kind.

"I've had enough nonsense about autograph albums for one evening," Mr. Wilkins went on. "And if anyone else comes knocking at the door interrupting me, I'll—I'll . . . Well, they'd better not do it "

"Yes, sir . . . No, sir." Atkinson sidled out of the room, thankful to make his escape from the indignation of L. P. Wilkins, Esq.

Upstairs in the library he met Darbishire and Temple. "Phew! I'm not having any more of this caper," he complained. "Sir's just about ready to go off like an H-bomb."

"He wasn't too bad when I was in there," Temple remarked. "I just asked for his autograph and . . ."

"You did *what*?"

"Asked for his autograph. It was the only thing I could think of."

"You might have had enough sense not to do that. You knew jolly well *I'd* bagged the album excuse."

"No, I didn't. You never told me. D'you mean to say *you* asked for his signature, too?"

"Yes, of course I did," said Atkinson. "No wonder he thought there was something funny going on with both of us giving the same excuse."

Darbishire looked at his fellow conspirators with deep reproach. "Not only *both* of you—all *three* of us," he said. "We seem to have bished things up properly. I only hope old Jennings has got something a bit more original up his sleeve for when it's his turn."

"Perhaps we ought to warn him," Temple suggested. "Let's go and see if we can find him before it's too late."

It already *was* too late. For when the three boys reached the common room they learned upon inquiry that Jennings had started off on his mission some two minutes earlier and was presumably making his way to the staff room by an alternative route.

"Well, that's that, then. There's nothing more we can do about it," Atkinson said, with a shrug. "I only hope it keeps fine for him."

The clock on the staff room mantelpiece stood at ten to eight when, for the fourth time in twenty minutes, a knock sounded on the staff room door.

Mr. Wilkins was annoyed. "Come in!" he shouted with the full force of his lungs. But no one entered in response to the invitation; for Jennings, unlike his fellow conspirators, was quick to realise that as the room was obviously occupied it would be more sensible to beat a retreat without divulging his identity.

Mr. Wilkins shouted again. Then he rose from his chair, crossed the room in three strides, and flung the door wide open. He was just in time to see a hurrying figure disappearing round the bend of the corridor.

"Stop! Come back, that boy!" he boomed in a voice that made the windows rattle.

After a short pause Jennings reappeared. He approached with casual footsteps as though taking an evening stroll.

"Did you call me, sir?" he inquired.

"Yes, I did. Was that you knocking at the staff room door?"

Jennings knitted his brows in thought. "Do you mean just now, sir?"

"Of course I mean just now. You don't think I meant the term before last, do you?"

"No, sir. Well, actually, I did just sort of tap on it, as you might say, sir."

"Then what on earth did you run away for instead of coming in when I told you to?"

"I—er—I changed my mind at the last moment, sir. I decided not to bother."

"What! Well, of all the——"

"I mean, I decided not to bother *you*, sir," the boy amended. "You see, I was going to ask you to write something in my autograph album. Nothing much, really. Just something like, *By hook or by crook . . .*"

"*Doh!*" A strangled cry of exasperation forced its way through Mr. Wilkins' vocal chords. He clasped his hands to his head and rocked gently from side to side. "This is the last straw!" he thundered when he had rocked himself to a standstill. "I've had enough of this ridiculous nonsense! And if you're not out of my sight in two seconds, Jennings, then by hook or by crook you'll be first in the detention book!"

"Yes, sir." Obediently Jennings backed away, and then turned and scampered round the bend of the corridor. When he reached the safety of the tuck box room he sat down on the hot-water pipes and heaved a sigh of disappointment. His first plan had gone sadly astray, but he was not giving up hope. All being well there might still be time to devise an alternative scheme.

As Mr. Wilkins turned to go back into the staff room he met Mr. Hind crossing the hall on his return from his tour of duty.

"Finished marking your books already?" his colleague inquired.

Mr. Wilkins shook his head. "I think I'll wait till morning. There are too many interruptions at this time of day."

"I shouldn't leave it too long," Mr. Hind observed. "After what you said about the Head wanting your form placings, I should get them through to him to-morrow morning by hook or by crook if I were you."

Mr. Wilkins winced and drew in his breath sharply. "Will you please *not* use that idiotic expression, Hind," he said warmly. "I've had enough hookery-crookery, not to mention jiggery-pokery, in the last twenty minutes to last me quite a long time!"

He turned on his heel and strode into the staff room. The door slammed loudly behind him.

CHAPTER 12

RECORD PERFORMANCE

THE failure of the secret mission to the staff room left Jennings' supporters in a despondent frame of mind. In the dormitory that evening he did his best to encourage them to make a further attempt, but his suggestion was greeted with grunts of disapproval.

"No jolly fear. I've had enough of that caper," Atkinson complained as he wriggled out of his pull-over. "I've been blown up once already by Old Wilkie because of you and your famous drawing, and I don't want a second helping, thanks very much."

Jennings pulled a long face. "It's all very well for you, Atki. But if you were in *my* place, and it was *your* geog book we wanted to get hold of——"

"Well, we've done our best," Temple broke in. "From now on it's up to you, Jen. You can't expect us to go on running ghastly risks for the rest of our lives, just for your sake."

Even Darbishire's loyalty wilted at the thought of having to brave Mr. Wilkins' wrath a second time. He was willing, he explained, to go to great lengths to help his friend. At the same time there must be a limit to his self-sacrifice; and to Darbishire's way of thinking, Mr. Wilkins was certainly the limit!

"I'll keep watch for you if you decide to have another bash," he volunteered. "But what with Old Wilkie sticking around the place like a watch dog. I'm not going in again by myself."

"But there's no *time* to have another bash," Jennings objected, waving one sock distractedly in the air. "For all we know he may be marking the wretched test at this moment."

Darbishire shook his head. "No, he won't. He told me he probably wouldn't be doing them until tomorrow, what with all the interruptions he was getting. If I were you I'd have another shot first thing in the morning."

As he lay in bed after the light had been put out, Jennings grappled with the problem that faced him. If what Darbishire said was correct, there was still a chance that the drawing could be erased before breakfast. At first glance this seemed an excellent moment to carry out the operation, for none of the masters would be downstairs at such an early hour. On the other hand, this was the time scheduled for his piano practice. In the adjoining room

Mr. Wilkins would be getting dressed, and would be sure to notice if the flow of music was interrupted for more than a few moments. If only he could think of some way of allaying the master's suspicions for just long enough to enable him to pay a quick visit to the staff room. If only . . . !

Suddenly Jennings caught his breath and sat bolt upright as a brilliant idea flashed into his mind. "Why, of course! With a little help from Darbishire he could devise a foolproof method of covering his absence from the piano stool.

In a hoarse whisper he called to his friend who was composing himself for slumber in the neighbouring bed. "Hey, Darbi, wake up! I've just had a fabulous wheeze!"

"Uh?" came in sleepy tones from under the blankets.

"It's about rubbing out that drawing. I couldn't think how to do it and then suddenly it came to me in a flash. Just like that. *Bingo!*" He paused, overcome by the sheer brilliance of his brainwave.

"Well, go on," yawned Darbishire. "What happened after Bingo came to you in a flash?"

"Well, Old Wilkie always bangs on the wall if I stop practising for more than a tenth of a second, so I thought if I could get someone to go on playing Beethoven's 'Minuet in G' for me while I nip down to the staff room——"

"Huh! If you're expecting me to play it you can start thinking all over again," Darbishire objected. "I've only got up to 'The Jolly Sailor Boy' in *Easy Pieces for Little Fingers.*"

"No one's asking you to play it! What I'm trying to tell you is that there's a gramophone record of that piece in the music room."

"What, 'The Jolly Sailor Boy'?"

"No, you clodpoll. Beethoven's 'Minuet in G.' Mr. Hind played it to me during my music lesson some weeks ago, so all you've got to do is——"

"Hey! Silence over there! Shut up nattering and go to sleep."

The tones of Bromwich, the dormitory prefect, cut

117

sharply across the explanation and Jennings was obliged to stop talking. Not that it mattered much, he told himself, because there was really no need for further discussion. Old Darbi would soon find out what he had to do when the time came to put the plan into operation.

At half-past seven the next morning Jennings entered the music room and began to thump out a spirited rendering of the Beethoven minuet. After a few bars he ceased playing and listened to make sure that Mr. Wilkins was keeping his usual check on what was happening in the adjoining room. Sure enough there came a sharp tapping on the wall—the customary signal to stop wasting time and proceed with the practice.

Jennings smiled to himself as he turned back to the keyboard. So far, the plan was going well.

Five minutes later an anxious-looking Darbishire poked his head round the door of the music room. "Here I am," he announced in a stage whisper. "What have I got to do?"

"Hop over to that cupboard in the corner," Jennings replied, breaking off in the middle of a bar. "There's a rack full of gramophone records on the top shelf, and somewhere amongst them you'll find one of the 'Minuet in G'."

"I still don't see why you can't do it yourself," Darbishire complained as he opened the cupboard. As though in answer to his query an impatient tapping sounded on the other side of the wall.

"*That's* why I can't do it myself," Jennings replied, hastily continuing with his practice. "It may take a little while to get the thing going and Sir hardly gives me time to turn over, let alone go scouting round for gramophone records."

After a short search, the unwilling disc jockey found the record and placed it on the turntable. Then he switched on the record player and held the pick-up arm poised above the grooves. "Say when," he commanded in a hoarse whisper.

Jennings stopped playing and jumped to his feet. "Okay! Start now," he ordered.

118

Immediately, the sound of the 'Minuet in G' was wafted once again round the music room. There was, admittedly, a difference in the quality of the playing, for the piece had been recorded by a pianist of international repute whose style and touch were of a somewhat higher standard than the usual *thump-pause-thump* rendering favoured by John Christopher Timothy Jennings. But this distinction was lost on the two boys. For them, the very fact that Beethoven's music continued to ring out after Jennings had left the piano stool caused them to flip their fingers with delight at the outstanding success of the experiment.

"Super, isn't it?" crowed Darbishire. "It sounds just like you playing. I bet Old Wilkie will be pleased. He'll think——"

"Don't waste time nattering, Darbi. I've got a job to do." Jennings made for the door. "I'll probably be back before the record's finished, but if I'm not, just start it playing over again."

He flashed an encouraging smile at his assistant and hurried from the room. The sound of Beethoven's 'Minuet in G' followed him along the corridor and down the stairs towards the staff room.

If Mr. Wilkins had been a little more alert he would not have been deceived for one moment by the altered style of playing emanating from the room next door. But three weeks of enforced listening to the daily practice had blunted his musical appreciation so much that he no longer listened with a critical ear, and was conscious of the music only when it stopped. Thus it was that the record player had been playing for nearly half a minute before he became aware that something unusual was afoot.

Tumpty-tumpty-tumpty-tumpty-tum. To his surprise he found himself humming the melody—a thing he had never done before. He paused in the act of buttoning his jacket and his brows narrowed in a puzzled frown. The music sounded quite different. Never before had he been able to hum in time with Jennings' thumping, uneven rhythm. There was no doubt about it: the boy was improving!

Still humming, still frowning, Mr. Wilkins stepped out on to the landing where he met Mr. Carter on his way downstairs to sort out the post.

"I say, come and listen to this," Mr. Wilkins greeted him. "For weeks that boy, Jennings, has been sending me out of my mind with a particularly unmusical version of the 'Minuet in G'."

"I'm not surprised," replied Mr. Carter. "From what Hind says about Jennings' progress I don't think he's got much faith in him as a musician."

"Well, he's wrong. The boy's a musical prodigy," Mr. Wilkins declared. "Listen to the way he's playing now."

Mr. Carter was not so easily misled. He listened for three bars and then said: "You're not trying to tell me that that's Jennings playing the piano?"

Mr. Wilkins nodded. "Amazing, isn't it?"

"It's more than amazing—it's impossible."

"Oh, come now, Carter, give the boy his due," Mr. Wilkins said generously. "I've often noticed how some of these boys seem to be making no progress at all. And then, quite suddenly . . ."

And then, quite suddenly, an unfortunate thing happened. The gramophone needle stuck in a worn groove and went on repeating the same notes over and over again.

It was, of course, the duty of Darbishire to see that no hitch of this sort occurred to mar the performance, but by some mischance he was on the far side of the room looking out of the window when the disaster took place. With a gasp of horror he rushed over to the record player and released the needle from its groove. . . . But by then it was too late.

"What—what . . . Good heavens! It's unbelievable!" Mr. Wilkins expostulated.

"On the contrary, Wilkins. It was obvious if only you'd listened carefully," Mr. Carter pointed out.

"Doh! If that silly little boy thinks he can sit there wasting his time listening to records instead of doing his practice . . ."

Leaving the sentence unfinished, Mr. Wilkins hurled open the music room door. "Jennings!" he shouted. "What's the meaning of——?"

And then he stopped; for there was no sign of Jennings anywhere in the room. Instead, a panic-stricken disc jockey, covered with guilty confusion, was vainly trying to conceal himself behind the cupboard door.

"Darbishire! What are you doing in here?" Mr. Wilkins demanded.

"I was just—er—I was just listening to the music," came the faltering reply.

"Oh, were you? And where's Jennings?"

Darbishire looked helplessly round the room as though half-expecting to find the missing pianist camouflaged as a 'cello case among the stack of instruments in the far corner. "He—er—he's not here, sir," he was forced to admit.

"I can see that, you silly little boy! What I want to know is where he's gone to."

Darbishire gulped slightly and mumbled: "He had to go downstairs, sir."

"Oh, did he!" A sudden suspicion flashed into Mr. Wilkins' mind. "To the staff room?"

There was no evading the direct question. Darbishire nodded unhappily.

"I see!" So there *was* some funny business going on, Mr. Wilkins decided. All that nonsense about autograph books the previous evening had been part and parcel of some fantastic plot to enable Jennings and his friends to pay an unlawful visit to the masters' common room. Why they should want to do so Mr. Wilkins didn't know. . . . But he was determined to find out!

With a curt order to Darbishire to return to his dormitory, the master withdrew from the music room and reported his findings to his colleague.

"Jennings, as usual!" he said angrily. "He's left the record player on as an alibi while he gets up to some sort of mischief downstairs."

"I imagined something like that was going on," Mr. Carter replied. "Aren't you going to investigate?"

"I certainly am!" Mr. Wilkins strode off along the corridor with a determined air. He'd soon put a stop to this nonsense, he told himself as he hurried down the stairs two at a time.

Meanwhile, Jennings was encountering unforeseen difficulties in the staff room. He had been expecting to find Form 3's geography books neatly stacked upon one of the shelves, but to his disappointment they were nowhere to be seen. With mounting anxiety he began to search, but it was not until nearly two minutes had ticked away that he came across the books half-hidden by a newspaper on the floor behind an armchair.

He knelt down and flipped his way through the pile, scanning the names on the covers—Venables, Bromwich, Martin-Jones, Atkinson—until he came across the object of his search: "J. C. T. Jennings," announced the cover of the last book but one, in wobbling capitals. Hurriedly he withdrew it from the pile, and was searching through his pockets for his india-rubber when he heard the sound of heavy footsteps approaching along the corridor.

Jennings caught his breath in alarm. Escape was impossible. If anyone should come into the room he would be caught red-handed without the slightest vestige of an excuse to offer. Perhaps the heavy footsteps would go on past the door. Perhaps . . . !

But Fate was against him; for at that moment the door swung open and L. P. Wilkins, Esq., M.A. (Cantab.) marched noisily into the room.

"Jennings! Just as I thought!" The master glared at the crouching figure beside the armchair. "Come along now. Out with it. What's the game?"

"Nothing, really, sir," the boy stammered as he rose to his feet. "At least, nothing much. I just wanted my geography book back before you marked the test, sir."

"Oh, did you! And I told you yesterday that you couldn't have it."

"I know, sir. Only I made a bit of a bish—er—a mistake, I should say. You see, I wasn't in the room when the books were collected, and Bromwich took mine out of my desk before I'd——"

The master glared at the crouching figure.

"All right, that's enough. Give the book to me. I think I'd better investigate this mistake for myself."

If the boy had been hoping to gain more marks by altering any of his answers, Mr. Wilkins was prepared to deal with the matter with the utmost severity. He thumbed his way through the pages, while Jennings watched in an agony of apprehension. At any moment the unflattering portrait would come to light. . . . But oddly enough it didn't!

When he reached the final page Mr. Wilkins handed the book back with a slight frown. "This isn't the right book," he said. "There's no geography test in this one."

For a second Jennings was mystified. Then he glanced down at the cover and noticed that the volume in his hand was, in fact, his *old* geography book that he had filled up the previous week. Obviously Bromwich, when rummaging through his desk, had picked up the first geography book that had come to hand, without bothering to inspect the contents. . . . And then in a flood of understanding came the realisation that his new book, which he had used for the test, must still be in his desk. *And that was the book in which he had drawn the cartoon of Mr. Wilkins!*

Jennings' first reaction was a feeling of heartfelt relief. All the anxiety he had suffered; all the schemes he had been impelled to devise! And he need never have bothered if only he had looked in his desk instead of jumping to hasty conclusions!

At this point he became aware that Mr. Wilkins was regarding him curiously. He pulled himself together and said: "Yes, sir, this is my *old* book. Bromwich collected it by mistake. May I go and get the proper one that I did the test in, please, sir?"

"Yes, you'd better, if you want any marks for it," said Mr. Wilkins. The puzzled frown deepened on his brow. Boys were extraordinary creatures, he thought, and their antics were quite beyond the power of adult understanding. Why couldn't the silly little boy have admitted in the first place that the wrong book had been given in, instead of contriving all this pantomime of autograph albums and record players to cover up a simple mistake. It was, of course, to his credit that he was anxious not to lose marks by failing to hand in the proper book; but the fantastic way he had gone about it left Mr. Wilkins in despair of ever following the workings of the juvenile mind.

"Go and get it at once," the master went on. "And I only hope you're going to keep your new book more tidily than your old one. I'm tired of seeing blots and scratchings out on nearly every page."

"Oh, yes. I'll see it's tidy, sir," Jennings said as he made for the door. His fingers closed reassuringly on the india-rubber in his trouser pocket. In the solitude of the classroom he would be able to erase every trace of the assistant masterpiece before he brought the book along to Mr. Wilkins. "Yes, sir. I'll go through it ever so carefully, and make quite sure it's all clean and neat and ready to be marked, sir."

CHAPTER 13

TOKEN OF GOODWILL

JENNINGS' mood was thoughtful as he walked back along the corridor after taking his geography book to Mr. Wilkins. The alarms and excursions of the previous evening—to say nothing of the nerve-racking ordeal he had just endured in the staff room—had subdued his usual high spirits. He gave a little shudder and blinked hard three times to blot out the memory of his narrow escape. After that he felt better, and able once again to turn his attention to more pleasant matters—the decorations for the Christmas party, for instance.

From the moment that he had suggested festooning the common room with paper chains, the craze had been growing more popular with the younger members of the school. In Form 1 the keenest interior decorators were Binns and Blotwell who spent a great deal of time experimenting with jam jars labelled *Home-brewed White-*

wash. This mixture, prepared from a secret formula invented by Binns, consisted of cold water and chalk dust with which he was proposing to camouflage the potted plants on his classroom window-sill as frost-covered Christmas trees. Tufts of cotton-wool were to be suspended above the flower-pots to give the impression of falling snowflakes, and the whole panorama was to be illuminated (Chief Electrician: R. G. Blotwell) with fairy lights constructed from torch bulbs covered with red blotting-paper.

In Form 3 the output of material had already surpassed the designer's original plan. During the past week the writhing coils of coloured paper had been growing longer and longer, so that it was becoming more and more diffi-

cult to cram the home-made decorations into the common room lockers where, on Mr. Carter's instructions, they were to be stored until the day of the party.

Something would have to be done about all this, Jennings decided as he joined the queue of boys waiting to go into the dining-hall for breakfast: if the preparations were allowed to continue unchecked the project would soon be completely out of hand.

At the tail end of the queue he found Darbishire hopping from foot to foot in nervous apprehension.

"What happened, Jen? Did you get your book back? Did Sir come in and catch you?" he twittered.

Jennings nodded. "Yes, he did, but it didn't matter after all."

"Didn't matter! But what about——?"

"Bromo gave in my old book by mistake—the one without the drawing in."

"Phew! Thank goodness for that!" Darbishire fanned himself and sagged at the knees with exaggerated relief. "I just didn't know what to do. You see, the record got stuck in a groove and Sir came prancing in and——"

"Yes, well never mind. That's all settled now." Jennings dismissed the subject with a wave of his hand. "What's worrying me at the moment is this business of decorating the common room. I should think we must have made at least half a mile of paper chain already."

"Let's measure it and see," Darbishire cried excitedly as the queue moved forward into the dining-hall. "Let's stretch it out in a straight line and go along it with a ruler." Then the practical difficulties of such a feat occurred to him and he added: "We'd have to do it when the wind wasn't blowing or we should be in a mess. Or perhaps we could let it down out of the dorm window and count the links as they went past, and multiply them by——"

"You're crazy. We couldn't possibly do it that way," Jennings objected. "You might as well say, why not let's get hold of a four-minute miler and see if he could run all the way along it in two minutes."

Darbishire's fancy was taken with this novel substitute for a foot-rule, and he spent the first half of the meal devising other equally fantastic methods of measuring time and distance. Finally he said: "It's a pity we've got to stop making more decorations. I was hoping to do a

127

rather artistic fringe to hang round the common room lampshade."

"Well, just do that and then pack up," Jennings conceded.

"I can't. I've scrounged through all the waste-paper baskets and there just isn't any more paper anywhere."

As usual, Jennings was able to recommend a way out of the difficulty. "You could use my old geog book for that—the one Sir's just given me back," he suggested.

"Don't you want it?" Darbishire queried hopefully.

"No, not really. It's bung full of old notes and stuff that I probably shan't need any more, so why not use it up for something useful."

"Good idea!" Darbishire agreed.

As it happened it was *not* a good idea; though it was not until some ten days later that Jennings realised what an ill-advised suggestion he had made.

As the end of term approached it brought with it the usual feeling of restless excitement. In out-of-school hours, masters were busy writing reports and checking equipment, while the boys were just as fully occupied in gathering together and packing their possessions in readiness for the holidays.

It was while he was clearing out his tuck box on the day before the end of term party, that Jennings remembered an important task which still remained to be done.

"Wow! I'd almost forgotten," he exclaimed to Venables, who was scraping the old labels from his tuck box on the other side of the room. "Old Wilkie's never given me back that penknife that he confiscated during the geog test."

"You'd better do something about it pretty quickly, then," Venables advised. He looked up from his scraping and frowned. "I know what I'd do if it was mine. I'd march into the staff room and ask him for it straight out. I'd soon show you I wasn't frightened of Old Wilkie."

"H'm!" said Jennings. It was all very well for Venables to talk of braving Mr. Wilkins' wrath in this easy fashion; but, then, it wasn't *his* penknife! Perhaps the wiser course would be to make his request at a time when the master was likely to be in a favourable frame of mind.

"I'll go after lunch," he decided. "It's that rather decent sponge pudding to-day, so there's a chance he'll be in a good mood by then."

Unfortunately Mr. Wilkins was *not* in a good mood during the hour after lunch. And when Mr. Carter entered the staff room shortly after two o'clock to collect Form 3's reports, he found his colleague searching through the table drawer in a state of mounting frustration.

"It's no good, Carter. I haven't even started those wretched reports yet—let alone finished them," Mr. Wilkins said irritably. "A most unfortunate thing's happened. I can't find my fountain pen anywhere."

"You couldn't have chosen a worse moment to lose it." Mr. Carter perched himself on the corner of the table. "The Head wants those reports finished as soon as possible. Are you sure you've looked properly?"

"Of *course* I've looked properly," Mr. Wilkins fumed, scattering the contents of the drawer from side to side and spilling the overflow on to the hearthrug. "I've looked everywhere. I can't think where on earth the thing's got to. I know I had it when I checked the stationery cupboard yesterday morning, but since then it's completely disappeared."

There was, indeed, some reason for Mr. Wilkins' annoyance, for with so much work waiting to be done he could ill afford to waste time searching for missing possessions. The prospect of having to complete his reports with a borrowed pen which might not suit his style of handwriting did not appeal to him in the least.

Thus, in spite of Jennings' hope that a generous portion of sponge pudding would soften Mr. Wilkins' heart, the master was not in the best of tempers when a knock sounded on the door a few minutes later.

Mr. Carter opened the door. "Well, what is it, Jennings?"

"Sir, please, sir, may I speak to Mr. Wilkins?"

"I very much doubt it. Mr. Wilkins is very busy at the moment. He's looking for his fountain pen."

"Oh!" There was a short pause and then: "Is it a red one with two gold bands round the cap that he's lost, sir?"

Mr. Wilkins looked round in sudden hope. "Yes, that's right! Have you seen it?" he asked eagerly.

"Oh, yes, I've seen it, sir."

"Thank goodness for that. Where is it, then?"

"I don't know, sir," Jennings replied as he advanced across the threshold. "I only meant I'd seen it—well, hundreds of times, in class and in your pocket and places like that."

Mr. Wilkins relieved his feelings with a short burst of *tut-tutting*.

"But if you can't find it, sir, you can borrow mine instead," Jennings hurried on. "I should be only too pleased to lend it to you, honestly, sir."

The generous offer caused a slight shudder to pass through Mr. Wilkins' powerful frame. The last time he had seen Jennings using a pen, the implement had consisted of two inches of well-chewed penholder wired on to a crossed nib which clicked like a turnstile and sent a spray of ink all over the paper. Politely but firmly, he declined the loan.

"I was only trying to do you a favour, sir," the boy persisted. "Because, you see, I was rather hoping you'd do me one back, sir."

"Can't you see I've no time for favours?" Mr. Wilkins retorted as he rummaged through a pile of magazines on the bookshelf. "Can't you see I'm busy?"

Jennings made a last determined effort to broach the subject of his visit. "It wouldn't take you a minute, honestly, sir," he pleaded. "You see, I was only wondering if you'd very kindly give me back my penknife that you confiscated, sir."

A frown of disapproval settled on Mr. Wilkins' brow. In point of fact he had every intention of returning the confiscated property before the boys dispersed for the holidays. At the same time, he was certainly not going to put himself out at the whim of an eleven-year-old third former. He would return the penknife when it suited him, and not before.

"For goodness' sake, boy, don't come bothering me with stupid nonsense about penknives when I've got more important things to think about." Mr. Wilkins pointed to the door. "Out!" he barked.

As he closed the staff room door behind him, Jennings puffed out his cheeks in aggrieved protest. Why couldn't Old Wilkie be decent considering it was nearly the end of term! From the way he had spoken, it didn't sound as though he meant to give the penknife back at all! Such a tragedy must be prevented at all costs. Somehow or other a way must be found of melting Mr. Wilkins' hard heart before it was too late.

For some moments after Jennings had taken his leave, the only sound in the staff room was a series of bumps and thuds as Mr. Wilkins struggled to move the bookcase away from the wall in the hope of finding his fountain pen behind it. When it was obvious that the search was fruitless, Mr. Carter cleared his throat in the apologetic manner of one who is about to announce an unpopular item of news.

"I'm sorry to bother you when you've already got so much to do, Wilkins," he began, "but the Head asked me to have a word with you about the end of term party tomorrow. He thinks it would create the right sort of festive spirit if we started the proceedings with a surprise item."

Mr. Wilkins paused in his efforts to return the bookcase to its usual position. "What sort of surprise?" he demanded.

"Oh, nothing very sensational," Mr. Carter replied in casual tones. "He just thought that if you were to come in to tea dressed as Father Christmas——"

"What!" Mr. Wilkins wheeled round in horrified protest. *"Me!* Father Christmas! Well, I—I . . . Dash it all, I mean . . ."

"It's perfectly simple. I've done it myself several times
131

in the past," his colleague assured him. "We've got the complete outfit upstairs in the theatrical cupboard—red robe, white whiskers, and all the usual trimmings."

"I dare say we have, but . . . Well, why can't *you* be Father Christmas if you're so keen on the idea? Considering you've done it before, you should be quite good at it."

But Mr. Carter was not to be persuaded. He would be busy organising the party, he pointed out. Indeed, it would be one of his duties to announce during tea that an important visitor had arrived. "That will be your cue to come marching in from the kitchen, smiling benevolently through your whiskers," he explained. "After that, you cut the cake and hand it round, wish everyone a merry Christmas and generally make yourself the life and soul of the party."

It was clear that Mr. Wilkins was not entirely happy about the rôle he was to play. "But what about my reports?" he objected.

Mr. Carter dismissed the objection with a shrug. "You won't be writing your reports during the party—even if you *have* found your pen by then. And if it doesn't turn up, I'll lend you mine. It's somewhat more reliable than the one Jennings offered you!"

Unable to think of any more excuses Mr. Wilkins said: "Oh, all right then, I'll play Father Christmas if you insist. Though why anyone should think that I've nothing better to do on the last day of term than to go traipsing round the building in fancy dress and ridiculous whiskers, I really can't imagine!"

Jennings was still trying to devise some means of putting Mr. Wilkins into a favourable frame of mind when he reached the common room a few minutes later. Here he found Darbishire at work on yet another Christmas card. For the past week he had been devoting most of his spare time to making decorations of one sort or another; and now that the paper chains and lampshade fringes were completed, he had returned to his original hobby of making cards to send to his friends and relations.

The latest example of Darbishire's art showed a stage coach trundling through snow considerably deeper than its axles. Along the top of the picture was a decorative border of Christmas puddings which, owing to an error in perspective, seemed to be issuing from the driver's coaching horn, giving the impression that he was blowing bubbles of unusual size. Underneath this scene was a sample of Yuletide poetry without which, in Darbishire's opinion, no Christmas card was really complete.

> "A Merry Xmas with lots of good cheer.
> From yours truly, C. E. J. Darbi-SHIRE,"

it announced in wobbling letters of blue crayon.

"Looks a bit weedy to me," was Jennings' comment as he peered over the artist's shoulder. "All that old-fashioned stuff about stage coaches and snow is miles out-of-date, these days."

"But you *have* to have snow on Christmas cards," Darbishire demurred. "It's pretty well compulsory."

"That's only because you always do such ancient moth-eaten pictures about ye olden days," Jennings replied scathingly. "You ought to see the modern slap-bang jet-propelled card that *I'm* drawing. Look, I'll show you."

So saying, he crossed to his locker and returned a few moments later with a sheet of paper which he had torn from his drawing-book the previous day. Though the picture was unfinished, it showed that the artist had scant respect for the kind of "oldë-worldë" greetings to which his friend was so devoted.

"That's not a Christmas card!" Darbishire protested as he studied the unfamiliar design. "Where's the snow? Where's the holly? Where are the plum puddings and robins and things?"

"You don't have to have them on jet-propelled ones," Jennings explained, seating himself at the table. "You see, this is a picture of a space-ship on the moon on Christmas day in the future—at least, it *will* be when it's finished."

"Oh, I see." Somewhat grudgingly Darbishire was forced to admit, on second thoughts, that there was

133

something to be said for this modern treatment of Yuletide scenes. Indeed, he wished he had thought of it himself; after all, a space-ship was much easier to draw than a coach and horses. He looked with interest as Jennings pointed out a cluster of spindly-legged creatures grouped in pairs, with their heads encased in goldfish bowls. At first he thought they were taking part in a tug-o'-war with inadequate pieces of rope; but a closer inspection suggested that they were merely engaged in pulling Christmas crackers.

"These chaps are space pilots having a party on the Moon," Jennings announced.

Darbishire peered at the pleasure-seekers with deep suspicion. "What's inside the crackers?" he demanded.

"How should I know? Paper hats, I suppose."

"You couldn't wear a paper hat on top of a space helmet. It'd blow away."

"Of course it wouldn't," Jennings replied knowingly. "There's no air on the moon to blow it with."

For a moment Darbishire seemed satisfied with this logical argument. Then he jabbed an accusing finger at the word *BANG* inscribed in block capitals above the heads of the merry-makers.

"Well, in that case, they wouldn't be able to hear the crackers going off, so that proves you're wrong," he crowed in triumph. "If I were you, Jen, I'd make them wear their paper hats *underneath* their space helmets instead of on top. After all, you want to get it scientifically accurate, don't you?"

Jennings shrugged. "I don't see that it matters much. I was only drawing it for something to do," he said. "I'll probably put it in the waste-paper basket when it's finished, unless—unless . . ."

His words tailed away as a brilliant idea flashed into his mind. "I've got it!" he cried jumping to his feet. "Supersonic brainwave!"

Darbishire stared at him in surprise. "What's up now?"

"I've just had a fabulous wheeze of what to do with this card when I've finished it."

"What?"

"I shall send it to Old Wilkie. You see, he's got my penknife and he won't give it back."

The look of surprise on Darbishire's face turned to an expression of blank bewilderment. "You must be crazy!" he said severely. "If Sir's done a rotten trick like that he doesn't deserve a Christmas card at all—let alone a jet-propelled, futuristic one."

Patiently Jennings explained the motive for his friendly token of greeting. A Christmas card drawn with painstaking care was a reminder that this was the season of goodwill. Such a timely hint would be sure to appeal to Mr. Wilkins' better nature so that, mellowed by kind thoughts, he would return the confiscated penknife without further argument.

"Not a bad scheme," Darbishire agreed as the plan was unfolded. "And you could—sort of—put jam on it with a lot of flannel about how he's always present in your thoughts at Christmas time."

That, in Jennings' opinion, was carrying things too far. "If you think I'm going to spoil my Christmas by thinking about Sir every minute of the day you're jolly well mistaken!" he declared.

"No, you don't *really* have to do that," Darbishire explained. "It's what they call poetic licence. For instance, underneath the picture you could write something like—er—let's see now . . ."

There was silence for a minute as the poet wrestled with his muse. Then he proudly announced: "How about this:

"Of wishing you well, I never will tire,
So the comps of the season to L. Wilkins, Esquire."

Jennings wrinkled his nose doubtfully. "What are comps?"

"Short for compliments," Darbishire translated. "That's a jolly decent thing to wish people at Christmas time." A thought occurred to him and he added: "After all, if he *doesn't* give you your knife back, you could easily send him an *un*complimentary one afterwards, cancelling all the kind thoughts."

135

"Yes, I suppose I could." A slow grin spread over Jennings' features. "Good old Darbi! The way you just rattle off poetry to order!"

The poet smiled modestly. "It comes to me in a flash— *Bingo!* Just like that," he said. "It's a gift, I suppose."

Frowning with concentration, Jennings settled down to finish the Christmas card. With the help of a little Yuletide spirit he now felt confident that he could win his way into Mr. Wilkins' favour.

CHAPTER 14

THE MISGUIDED MISSILE

THE ringing of the bell for the end of school the next morning was greeted by all the members of Form 3 with subdued squawks of delight. For it meant not only that lessons were over for the term, but also that they could start erecting their home-made decorations. Now, at last, the moment had arrived to bring forth the paper chains and makeshift ornaments which, on Mr. Carter's orders, they had stored out of sight pending the day of the party.

Needless to say the boys wasted no time in getting to work. As each locker door was flung open, a tightly packed coil of coloured paper came springing out like a jack-in-the-box. Soon the floor was littered ankle-deep with twisted chains, and as each boy struggled to unravel his tangled links from those of his neighbour, the room became a snake-pit of writhing activity.

As Jennings had predicted, there was no shortage of material. From end to end the common room was festooned with loops and folds of gaily-coloured streamers, so that the walls and ceiling were almost completely obscured. Various methods were devised to hold the chains in place: drawing-pins, stamp hinges, sticky tapes, tin tacks and even corn plasters were pressed into service in an effort to keep the decorations from cascading down on to the heads of the decorators. At last the work was finished and the boys were free to stroll round and admire the result of their labours.

"It looks ever so gay, doesn't it," said Temple, jumping down from Venables' shoulders after pinning a silver paper star to the bookcase. "In one way it's a pity we're going home tomorrow. All this effort, just so that we can look at it for half an hour or so before tea!"

"They ought to have let us put it up weeks ago; then we really should have had our money's worth," Venables replied. Honesty compelled him to add: "Of course, if we *had*, it might have been a bit of a job playing ping-pong and swapping stamps and things with all these streamers tickling the back of your neck all the time."

Shortly afterwards, Mr. Carter came into the common room to inspect the handiwork. He walked carefully so as not to disturb the strips of paper hanging precariously over his head, and others which—owing to the poor quality of the stamp hinges—kept wrapping themselves round his ears. He was thankful that the boys had devised this peaceful method of whiling away the last restless hours before the party. At least it kept them quiet.

As he approached the table by the window he noticed Jennings and Darbishire poring over a large sheet of drawing-paper. Jennings looked up as the master drew level.

"Sir, please, sir, were you alive in the olden days?" he asked.

Mr. Carter raised a suspicious eyebrow. But one glance at Jennings' earnest expression convinced him that the boy was not trying to be funny.

"I mean, can you remember what it was like years ago, when they used to have snow and stuff laid on for Christmas, sir?"

"I *can* remember seasonable weather at this time of year," Mr. Carter admitted. "Why do you ask?"

"Well, sir, I was having an argument with Darbishire about this Christmas card I'm doing. You see, it's an up-to-date, jet-propelled one, but Darbishire still says snow is compulsory, sir, and I wondered if there was any rule about it."

"No, Jennings—no rule," said Mr. Carter gravely.

"Oh, that's good, sir," said Jennings, relieved. He held up the sheet of drawing-paper for the master's inspection. "You see, I'm going to send it to Mr. Wilkins. I thought if I made him a specially decent one he might feel all Christmassy and give me my penknife back before we go home tomorrow."

The peace-offering designed to soften Mr. Wilkins' heart was certainly up-to-date—even, perhaps, a little in advance of its time. For now that the picture was finished it portrayed a space-suited Father Christmas crash-landing his flying saucer on the moon. In addition to the merry-making space pilots pulling their crackers, there was now a further group of lunar explorers engaged in the difficult task of eating their Christmas dinner without removing their plastic helmets. Above the domes of their pressurised headgear floated little balloons filled with seasonable conversation. *("A Merry Christmas, Profes-sor." . . . "Same to you. Pass the mince pies, old chap.")* As a concession to Darbishire's feelings about old-fashioned Christmas scenes, a robin was perched on a yule log in the middle distance.

"D'you think he'll like it, sir?" Jennings asked eagerly.

"It's jolly good, isn't it?" chimed in Darbishire, his spectacles athwart his nose like a percentage sign. "Of course I helped too, sir. The poem about the comps of the season was specially composed by me—copyright reserved, sir."

"H'm," mused Mr. Carter. "I doubt whether a flying saucer is *quite* Mr. Wilkins' cup of tea, but it may bring him down to earth on the subject of confiscated penknives."

"Oh, good-o, sir."

"And I'm sure he'll like the poem, Darbishire. He'll be delighted—and perhaps a little surprised—to hear that Jennings never tires of wishing him well."

The news of Jennings' intentions had already caused a certain amount of interest among the members of Form 3; and when Mr. Carter had gone, a group of boys gathered round the artist to inspect the final result of his work. Temple did his best to find fault with it.

"I thought you said there was no air on the moon," he challenged.

"That's right—there isn't. That's why they're all wearing space-helmets—even during dinner," Jennings explained.

"Well, what about that robin, then? He seems to be breathing all right."

The artist dismissed the criticism with a wave of his pencil. "You couldn't put a robin in a space-helmet—it'd look silly," he said. "Anyway, so long as it's Christmassy I don't suppose Sir will mind. He'll probably think it's holding its breath."

The next move was to send the card to Mr. Wilkins without delay. Jennings, as usual, had his own ideas about how this should be done.

"As it's a jet-propelled job I'm going to deliver it by air-mail," he announced.

The group stared in puzzled wonder as he crossed to the window and looked out . . . Yes, it *should* be possible to send a guided missile through the staff room window, he decided. In fact, it looked an easy target, for the staff room was on the ground floor barely ten yards away, and the wall ran at right angles to where he was standing at the common room window on the storey above.

Fortunately the window of the staff room was open at the top, and through the aperture Jennings could see Mr. Wilkins seated at the table, studying a book with close attention. A broad grin spread over the boy's face as he turned to his friends standing beside him.

"Come on, gather round the launching base for ye famous vertical jet-lift take-off," he announced.

"What's the big idea?" Venables demanded.

"I'm going to put a rocket into orbit round Sir's head. Well, not *quite*, but you'll see what I mean if you watch."

So saying, Jennings picked up the greetings card and carefully folded it into the shape of a dart. On one of its wings he wrote: *"To Mr. Wilkins, from J. T. C.*
139

Jennings." Then he opened the common room window and stood with the missile poised above the sill.

"Stand by for take-off!" he cried in tones of mock importance. "Contact! . . . Chocks away! . . . Port engine revving up . . . Clear the runway—she's off!"

Taking careful aim, he launched the missile on its maiden flight. The dart soared upwards, then spiralled across the intervening space losing height all the time.

"She'll never get into orbit. She's swerving," Atkinson exclaimed anxiously.

"It's all right; she's banking beautifully now," Temple reported. "Heading straight for the target area."

In breathless suspense the boys followed the flight. At one point it seemed certain that the dart would hit the wall wide of the window, but at the last moment it veered away and skimmed into the room a bare inch above the open sash.

"Hurray! Hurray! Direct hit!" cried Darbishire in wild excitement. "*Slap-bang-wallop* on the bull's eye!"

"Jolly good shot!" shouted Venables, thumping the missile designer between the shoulder blades in hearty congratulation.

"Ssh! Quiet! All get down out of sight," Jennings ordered. "It only just missed the top of his head and if he turns round and sees us grinning at him it'll spoil the surprise."

Accordingly the little group crouched low under the window, only Jennings remaining at a vantage point with his eyes just above the sill, where he could give his friends a running commentary on what was happening in the staff room below.

"He's picking it up off the floor," he announced in a stage whisper. "He's looking at it now."

"Is he reading my poem?" Darbishire queried hopefully.

"No, he's looking up at this window. He's guessed where it's come from after all."

"That's a good sign, anyway," said Atkinson. "I expect he'll come up to you during the party and say thank you in person."

He launched the missile on its maiden flight.

"And if he does you can round it off nicely by wishing him a few more of those comps of the season that Darbishire's always nattering about," Venables suggested.

It certainly seemed that the guided missile's maiden flight had been a great success.

"I bet old Sir will be ever so pleased," said Darbishire beaming with seasonable goodwill. "I bet it'll put him in such a festive mood that he'll give you your knife back with a sprig of holly on the top."

Jennings dodged quickly away from the window. "We'll soon know about that," he said. "He's just gone stonking out of the room, and I've got a feeling he's coming up here, right away."

Unfortunately, the jet-propelled greetings card failed to inspire Mr. Wilkins with feelings of goodwill, as Jennings had hoped. Indeed, it had the reverse effect, for his first reaction, as the missile sailed in through the window and skimmed the top of his head, was one of extreme annoyance. . . . Had these boys no manners! What did they think they were playing at, hurling pieces of paper into the staff room in this insolent manner?

He picked up the dart and glanced at it briefly—so briefly, in fact, that he did not see the inscription, nor even recognise the picture as a Christmas card designed in his honour. All the effort that had been put into the drawing seemed to him to be nothing more than childish scribble. What he *did* notice, however, was that the dart had been made from a page torn from a school drawing book.

Mr. Wilkins simmered with indignation. Only two days before, when checking the contents of the stationery cupboard, he had been appalled to learn what a large quantity of exercise books the boys had used during the term. The headmaster, too, had been equally concerned when the facts were reported to him. So much so, that during the breaking-up assembly that morning he had impressed upon the whole school the need for the strictest economy in future . . . And here were these disobedient boys wantonly wasting expensive drawing books by tearing

142

out pages and scattering them about as though they were taking part in a paper chase. . . . He would soon put a stop to this extravagant nonsense, Mr. Wilkins told himself, as he strode resolutely out of the staff room.

Meanwhile, on the floor above, the inventor of the aerial Christmas card was still enjoying the hearty back-slappings of his colleagues.

"I reckon Sir ought to feel jolly honoured," Darbishire was saying for the fifth time a few moments later. "Considering old Jennings has gone out of his way to be specially decent, I reckon he's bound to . . ."

He stopped abruptly as the common room door swung open to reveal the tall figure of Mr. Wilkins on the threshold. In his hand he held a crumpled dart, and it was clear from his expression that the jet-propelled greetings had aroused no answering echo in his heart. For a moment he glowered at the paper chains festooned like lines of washing from wall to wall. Then he said: "Which of you ill-mannered little boys has been throwing pieces of paper into the staff room?"

The group looked at him in dismay. This was no way to respond to friendly wishes of goodwill!

"Oh, but, sir, you don't understand . . ." Jennings began.

"So it was you, was it? Jennings, as usual," Mr. Wilkins broke in. "I might have known it! Really, your behaviour is deplorable. How dare you turn the masters' common room into a refuse dump by hurling half the contents of the waste-paper basket through the window!"

"That wasn't waste paper, honestly, sir," Jennings defended himself. "It was a sheet of my drawing book that I'd done a Christmas card on—specially for you, personally, sir."

"To put you in a good mood, sir," Darbishire added incautiously.

"What did you say, Darbishire?"

"Er—I mean, to wish you the comps of the season, sir. We thought you'd be ever so pleased."

For a moment Mr. Wilkins' icy disapproval seemed about to thaw. If the boys' motive really had been well-intentioned, then he was prepared to regard the matter in a different light. Even so, there was no excuse for tearing pages out of a drawing book so soon after the headmaster's warning about the extravagant use of school stationery.

"I see. I hadn't realised it was a Christmas card," he said in kindlier tones, as he advanced into the room. "Thank you very much! All the same, Jennings, you've been told often enough that exercise books are a very expensive item, and it's sheer, wasteful . . ."

At that moment an unfortunate thing happened. Seeking to underline his warning with a gesture, Mr. Wilkins made a wide sweep with his arm and touched a weak link in the paper chain suspended above his head. Immediately an endless coil of crinkly links cascaded down on to his shoulders like a victor's garland of flowers.

The boys stared aghast as he struggled to free himself from the embracing struggle of streamers.

"*Doh!* Why on earth you boys have to clutter the place up with all this ridiculous tomfoolery . . ." Mr. Wilkins fumed. He snatched at a length of chain which had twisted itself round his neck, and glared at the offending object with disfavour. He was about to let it drop to the floor when something about it caught his eye and he looked at it more closely. Like the rest of the home-made decorations, the piece which he held had been made from strips of paper cut, coloured and gummed to form the links of a chain. And underneath the blue and red crayon he could read a number of words and phrases which told him only too clearly where the material for the streamer had come from.

Wool is the chief product of Australia, one of the links informed him in spidery handwriting. *In New Zealand sheep are reared on the Canterbury Plains,* another announced; while a few feet farther along the chain, a fragment of the coast-line of South America suggested the previous existence of a sketch map.

Mr. Wilkins bridled indignantly. Here was proof that some boy had been using his geography notebook for a highly irregular purpose.

"What's the meaning of this?" he demanded. "How dare any of you boys tear up your exercise books to make these trumpery decorations?"

The little group fidgeted uncomfortably. "It's not my book, sir," Temple said virtuously.

"Nor mine, either, sir. I only used old newspapers and stuff," Atkinson volunteered.

"It's obviously *some* boy in Form 3," Mr. Wilkins went on. "Come along, now, have any of you others been tearing up your exercise books?"

Jennings gulped and swallowed hard. "Please, sir, I think that piece came from my book," he admitted.

"*Doh!* You silly little boy!"

"But it was only my *old* one, sir," Jennings explained, quite unaware that he had committed an offence. "It was all used up with old notes and stuff, so I didn't think it'd be wanted again as it was the end of term, sir."

Mr. Wilkins almost danced with frustration amongst the ruins of the home-made lampshade.

"Of *course* it'll be wanted again," he stormed. "The fact that a book is full of notes doesn't mean it can be thrown away. It's something to be kept and referred to all through your school life. . . . And here's a whole term's work on the geography of Australia, New Zealand and South America torn to shreds to make these absurd decorations!"

"I'm sorry, sir. I didn't think," Jennings confessed.

"You never *do* think, that's the trouble! What's the point of my dictating notes if you're going to tear the things up as soon as you've written them down!"

"Yes, sir. I mean, no sir. No good at all, sir."

By this time Jennings was well aware of the breach of rules he had unwittingly committed. However, the damage was done, now; and since he had apologised, surely the best thing to do was to consider the matter over and done with.

But Mr. Wilkins had other ideas. "You deserve to be severely punished for sheer wasteful extravagance of school stationery, to say nothing of destroying the notes of a term's work." He searched his mind for a fitting punishment. "And that being the case, you can stay away from the party this afternoon."

Gasps of horror and dismay rose up from the group at the severity of the sentence.

"Oh, *sir*, please let him off, sir," Darbishire pleaded. "After all, it *is* nearly Christmas, sir."

"Be quiet, Darbishire! I don't care if it's August Bank Holiday. You boys have got to learn that you can't play fast and loose with school rules and expect to get away with it."

Jennings stood numb with misery. This was the end of everything. All the trouble he had taken to inspire Mr. Wilkins with feelings of goodwill and now *this* had to happen! With an effort he forced his mind back to what the master was saying.

". . . and you can spend the time doing something useful instead. You can tidy the stationery cupboard and make sure all the books are stacked in apple-pie order."

Tearing himself free from the streamers entangling his ankles, Mr. Wilkins strode to the door. On the threshold he turned and said: "That's what we mean, Jennings, by letting the punishment fit the crime. If you're made to devote your energies to tidying the stationery cupboard, it may, perhaps, teach you not to tear up valuable exercise books quite so freely another time!"

There was a buzz of protest as Mr. Wilkins left the room.

"Coo! Weedy chizz! Jolly well not fair," fumed Darbishire.

"And after you'd gone to all that trouble specially to be decent to him," Venables sympathised. "He's as bad as that mouldy old chap in *A Christmas Carol*, who said Christmas was all humbug."

"He's *worse*, if you ask me," said Temple. "After all, old Scrooge got a bit of sense knocked into him in the end, but I reckon it'd take more than Marley's ghost to make Old Wilkie see reason."

Nods of approval greeted this observation. There was no doubt that all the boys felt a sense of injustice on their friend's behalf. After all, he had gone out of his way to

146

please Mr. Wilkins—and this was the result. And on the last night of term, too, when by rights the spirit of Christmas should have mellowed the heart of even the most churlish of schoolmasters.

The paper chains they had worked so hard to construct now seemed nothing but a mockery. What was the point of making the room look gay if the project was to end in disaster!

Jennings heaved a sigh of resignation as he turned to the door. "Oh, well! Better get on with it, I suppose," he said in a dull, flat voice.

CHAPTER 15

FALSE WHISKERS FOR TWO!

STRICTLY speaking, the stationery cupboard was not a cupboard at all. It was a small room at the end of the corridor adjoining Form 5b classroom. Two days previously, Mr. Wilkins had inspected the stock and compiled a list of requirements for the following term. He had not, however, had time to tidy the contents of the shelves when he had finished. Thus it was that when Jennings pushed open the door of the little room he found both floor and shelves piled high with stationery and books. In addition, rulers, pens, pencils, boxes of chalk and blotting-paper were strewn about waiting to be sorted into some semblance of order.

Grudgingly the boy set to work, but he had not been long at his task when Darbishire's face appeared round the edge of the door.

"I'll help you if you like, Jen," he volunteered. "Only till the party starts, of course—I don't want to miss that."

"Thanks, Darbi." Jennings was grateful: not so much for the help as for the feeling of sympathy which lay behind it. "It won't take long if we both get cracking. You sort out the arith books while I round up the rulers."

"Right-o. Of course, if there's anything decent to eat at the party I'll try and fox a bit out for you in my pocket," said Darbishire, stooping to prise a couple of nibs from the cracks between the floorboards. "I may have a bit of

147

a job with the jelly, but the cakes shouldn't be too difficult."

For some minutes they worked in silence, arranging the books in tidy rows and gathering together the straying rulers and rubbers.

And then Jennings made his great discovery. . . . Tucked away at the back of a shelf behind a box of chalk he came across a fountain pen. He knew to whom it belonged as soon as he saw it.

"Wow! Crystallised cheesecakes! Look what I've found! " he cried, waving the pen under his friend's nose.

Darbishire peered at the object with scant interest. "What about it? It's only an old one."

"But don't you know whose it is? Look at the two gold bands round the cap. It's Old Wilkie's!"

A closer inspection confirmed the discovery to Darbishire's satisfaction. "That's right. It's the one he always uses for marking our books."

"Yes, but that isn't all," Jennings pointed out. "He's been creating like a brace of foghorns for the last day or so because he couldn't find the thing. He's been searching high and low for it."

"Serves him right for being so careless. He's always moaning at us for leaving things about," Darbishire snorted as he replaced the pen on the shelf. "What rotten luck finding it for him just after he's been so gruesome. He jolly well doesn't deserve to get it back, if you ask me."

"Perhaps not, but—well, I can't very well confiscate it, like he confiscated my penknife," Jennings replied. "On the other hand, I wonder if . . ." He scratched his nose thoughtfully while he pondered his next move. If he returned the lost property forthwith, the grateful owner should, in theory, be so pleased that he would cancel the punishment he had imposed. . . . On the other hand, he might not! . . . What did Darbishire think?

"It's worth trying," his friend advised. "Let's go and find him right away. The party will be starting any minute now."

Hastily they bundled the rest of the books back on to

148

the shelves. By now the cupboard was at least outwardly tidy, and there was every chance that Mr. Wilkins would not bother to inspect the result of their labours too closely.

Jennings slipped the pen into his pocket and shut the cupboard door. As he did so a bright idea floated into his mind.

"Listen, Darbi, I've had a brainwave," he exclaimed, his eyes alight with inspiration. "I'm not going to take it to Old Wilkie just yet."

"Why not?"

"I've just thought of a way of making it more Christmassy, only I shall want your help."

"What, another of my Yuletide poems?" queried Darbishire. "Actually, I've got one almost ready: all about, *How jolly is ye holly*."

"No, not that sort of help. Come up to the dorm with me and I'll tell you all about it."

At that moment the school bell began to ring. All along the corridor, doors opened and boys came hurrying out on their way to the party in the dining-hall.

Darbishire was seized with a sudden anxiety. "But I can't come now. The bell's gone," he protested. "*I'm* going to the party, Jen, even if you're not."

"We'll *both* be going to the party if you do what I tell you." Seizing his friend by the arm Jennings steered him through the stream of party guests and hustled him up the stairs to Dormitory 4.

It was Venables' reference to *A Christmas Carol* that had given him the idea, Jennings explained when they reached the dormitory. Thanks to the Spirits of Christmas Past and Christmas Present, the churlish Scrooge had become a generous, kindly person when he found himself in the company of happy cheerful people intent on enjoying the festive season to the full. . . . Very well then! Why not subject Mr. Wilkins to the same treatment.

"What I mean is, it's no good giving Sir his pen back when he's in a bate. He'll just take it and say nothing," Jennings explained. "The proper time to do it is during tea. He'll be in a decent mood then, what with stuffing himself with mince pies and jelly and stuff."

Darbishire nodded. "Yes, of course. Wait till the feast has got going and then come marching into the dining hall and give him his pen as a—as a sort of Christmas present. Good scheme, Jen. He's bound to let you stay on for the rest of the party after that."

A broad grin spread over Jennings' features. "That's the general idea, Darbi, only"—he lowered his voice to a whisper of secrecy—"only it won't be *me* who comes marching in—it'll be Father Christmas!"

Darbishire looked blank. "Father Christmas!" he echoed.

"Oh, it'll be me, *really*—disguised, you see," Jennings went on excitedly. "When everybody's settled down, there'll be a sudden rat-tat-tat at the door." He beat a distinctive tattoo on the chest of drawers by way of demonstration. "Everybody will look round, and—hey presto! Enter me in a red robe and white whiskers. I shall walk straight up to Mr. Wilkins . . ."

"Wish him the comps of the season."

". . . and give him his pen back as a special present from Father Christmas."

The two boys beamed at each other in satisfaction. No one—not even Mr. Wilkins—could be so ill-mannered as to order Santa Claus from the room after such a demonstration of goodwill.

Then the smile faded from Darbishire's face and he said: "Yes, but look here: where are you going to get the disguise from? You haven't got much time, you know. They're lining up to go into the dining hall already."

Jennings, as usual, had a ready answer for all queries. Crossing to his bed he threw back the bedspread and revealed a bright red blanket beneath.

"*Voilà*," he said. "I can put it over my head and pin it under my chin so it hangs down all round. It'll look just like a Father Christmas cloak, won't it."

"H'm! *Something* like, I suppose," Darbishire said doubtfully. "What about your beard, though?"

150

"Cotton-wool. Matron's got masses in the sick room. And I can stick it on with—with——"

"With what? We used up all the stamp hinges on the decorations, don't forget."

Jennings solved the problem with a nod of his head. That's all right. I've got a tube of balsawood cement in my locker."

Darbishire frowned and pursed his lips. "Wow! You'll need sandpaper to get it off afterwards."

"Never mind afterwards: that can take care of itself." Impatiently, Jennings turned and made for the door. "Off you go and get some cotton-wool from Matron, while I fetch the balsa cement. Meet you back here in two minutes."

Whereupon, he led the way on to the landing and bounded down the stairs two at a time. There was not a moment to lose if his latest plan was to succeed. . . . And after so many failures, surely it was time that *something* would work out in his favour.

In fairness to Mr. Wilkins it must be said that he had no real intention of forbidding Jennings to attend the Christmas party. The ban which he had imposed in the heat of the moment was, in reality, more of a threat than a punishment—a sentence which could be repealed at the eleventh hour, thus giving an added joy to the reprieve. Moreover, he had decided to return the confiscated penknife before the boys went to bed as further proof that all schoolmasters have hearts of gold—well, on the last night of term, anyway! Indeed, he was actually on his way to the stationery cupboard in his rôle of fairy godfather when the bell rang for tea.

As the sound of the bell died away, Mr. Carter emerged from the dining-hall and hailed his colleague as he was about to climb the stairs.

"Come along now, Wilkins. It's time you were assuming your disguise," he said.

"Disguise?" For a moment Mr. Wilkins looked blank. Then he remembered Ah, yes, of course! That Father Christmas business. He had had so many things to attend to in the last few days that he had forgotten about the part which he had agreed to play: and now that he was reminded of it, he looked upon the project with certain misgivings.

"You know, Carter, I think it'd be much better if *you* were to be Santa Claus," he said persuasively. "I don't honestly think I'm cut out for the part."

"Nonsense! You'll be a roaring success," Mr. Carter replied in tones that permitted no argument. He took his colleague by the arm and guided him gently but firmly across the hall and into the staff room. . . . And thus it was that Mr. Wilkins' mind was turned to other matters, and he forgot all about his intention of finding Jennings and granting the last-minute reprieve.

"I thought it would be best if you were to dress up in here where the boys won't see you," Mr. Carter went on as he closed the staff room door. "I want to keep the whole thing a surprise until the right moment."

Laid out on the table were the scarlet robe and hood, while dangling on a piece of elastic from the cupboard door knob was a long white beard smelling strongly of moth balls.

Muttering to himself, Mr. Wilkins began struggling into his costume; but owing to his lack of patience with an unfamiliar garment, he soon became lost in its folds. With his head enshrouded in the fur-lined hood which came down over his eyes, he groped and tunnelled his way blindly through yards of material, until finally his left foot emerged through one of the armholes as his face appeared at the opening of the corresponding sleeve.

"This is fantastic. It must have been made for an octopus," he panted, drawing in a lungful of welcome fresh air.

Mr. Carter said: "Try again. You've got it on back to front and upside down; and I rather think it's inside out as well."

At his second attempt Mr. Wilkins succeeded in donning his costume. With an air of injured martyrdom he stretched over his head the elastic band to which his whiskers were attached. For a moment he stood with his

152

beard jutting straight out from his forehead, the ends drooping down a foot in front of his eyes like the fringe of a lampshade.

"Prickly stuff this crêpe hair—it tickles," he complained, wrinkling his nose against the smell of mothballs. He pulled the whiskers down over his face and found his nose protruding through the gap between the moustache and the beard. A muffled query came from behind the hairy screen. "I say, Carter, this doesn't seem quite right to me."

Patiently, Mr. Carter arranged the whiskers and adjusted the elastic band. "That looks splendid, Wilkins! You make a perfect Father Christmas," he declared, stepping back to admire the transformation.

"Glad you think so," Father Christmas grunted. "My goodness! These whiskers are warm; it's like wearing a scarf round your face. I tell you, I shall be glad when this party is over."

Mr. Carter ignored the criticism and proceeded to brief Father Christmas in his duties. "Stay here until all the boys have gone in to tea," he said. "Then go along to the kitchen and wait by the door leading into the dining-hall. You will be able to hear me announce that an important visitor has arrived and that's your cue to knock on the door. . . ."

"Like this," said Mr. Wilkins, beating out a distinctive rhythm of seven taps on the staff room table.

"That's the idea! Whereupon you'll make your entry and—well . . ." Mr. Carter spread his hands in a gesture of easy confidence as he turned to leave the room. "Well, after that the party should *really* get going."

In this respect Mr. Carter was right; even though he was unaware of certain plans which were, at that moment, taking shape in another part of the building.

CHAPTER 16

THE CHRISTMAS SPIRIT

IT was quiet upstairs in Dormitory 4, and although the rest of the school were down below in the dining-hall,
153

Jennings and Darbishire found themselves speaking in whispers.

"They've just sat down for tea. I heard the chairs rumbling," Darbishire confided as he teased out a roll of cotton-wool which he had found in Matron's dispensary.

Jennings nodded, and glanced at his reflection in the mirror. By now, he had the red blanket pinned under his chin and trailing round him in the form of an improvised cloak. "There isn't much balsa cement left, so I may have to help out with soap," he said.

Darbishire looked doubtful. "I only hope it doesn't drop off in the middle, that's all."

"Oh, it should be all right in the middle. It's the side pieces we'll have to be careful with."

"No, you clodpoll. I mean the middle of the party, not the middle of the whiskers." Darbishire picked up a pair of nail scissors and shaped the cotton-wool into a long spade-shaped beard. "Here you are, Jen. Try this for size."

The balsa cement proved to be an excellent substitute for spirit gum: so good, in fact, that the boys had a great deal of trouble with wisps of cottonwool adhering to their fingers as they struggled to fix the beard in place. Between them, however, they at last succeeded in festooning Jennings face in a fluffy cocoon of white whiskers of which both the make-up artists were extremely proud. As a precaution against accidents, Jennings looped a pyjama cord under his chin and knotted it on top of his head beneath the makeshift hood.

"Jolly good, Jen. You look as though you'd just flown in from the North Pole," Darbishire decided as he wiped his sticky fingers on the dormitory curtain. "And that red blanket suits you right down to the ground—so mind you don't trip over it."

Jennings' nose twitched like a rabbit's at the tickling touch of his cotton-wool moustache. "Phew! These whiskers are warm. It's like going about with your face wrapped up in a parcel," he said unconsciously echoing the same complaint that Mr. Wilkins had made a few minutes before.

As he followed his friend down the stairs, Jennings' mind was occupied with a last-minute rehearsal of his plan. He would wait outside until Darbishire had gone into the dining hall and made an excuse for his late arrival. Then he would knock loudly on the door—seven distinctive taps would be the best way of announcing his entry, he decided: after which he would fling wide the door . . . . A sudden spasm of stage fright assailed him and he clutched Darbishire's sleeve in panic and alarm.

"Oh, goodness, Darbi, supposing it doesn't work!" he quavered. "Supposing Old Wilkie gets into a bate! Supposing my whiskers drop off and everybody laughs."

"You'll be all right," his friend assured him. "Have you got the fountain pen?"

"Yes, it's in my pocket."

"That's all right, then. Keep your fingers crossed and hope for the best. You can't back out of it now." Darbishire hopped down the last three stairs and skipped along to the dining hall. As his hand rested on the knob he turned and beamed an encouraging smile at the pathetic-looking figure in the trailing red blanket.

"Best of luck, Jen," he called in a hoarse whisper. "And the comps of the season, too."

Jennings was feeling too nervous to reply. His rôle had seemed an easy one when he had first thought of the idea, but now that the moment for action had arrived his confidence had drained away and he was dreading the ordeal which lay before him.

He would have been surprised to learn that he was not the only person who was worrying about the part he had to play . . . . But then, he had no means of knowing that, at that moment, a red-robed and white-whiskered Mr. Wilkins was hiding behind the kitchen door ready to make his entry from the opposite end of the dining-hall.

It was not the custom at Linbury Court School to make elaborate preparations for the end of term party. There were, however, a few concessions to the festive season:

155

the dining-hall was decorated with a Christmas tree, and tea was supplied on a more generous scale than usual. After tea, there were games and carol singing followed by some sort of entertainment. Normally, this took the form of a concert organised by the boys, but on this occasion Mr. Pemberton-Oakes had decided to show a programme of films instead.

In spite of its modest aims, the party was the most eagerly awaited event of the autumn term; for it meant that work was over and done with, and the spirit of Christmas was in the air.

The party had been going for about ten minutes when Darbishire slipped unobtrusively into the dining-hall. With a garbled excuse to Mr. Carter to cover his late arrival, he hurried to his seat fearful lest his plate of ham and tomatoes would be whisked away before he had had time to eat it.

"Where on earth have you been?" demanded Venables, who was impatiently waiting for the next course to be served.

"Oh, nowhere special," Darbishire replied, cramming a forkful of ham into his mouth. "Or rather—I can't tell you now. It's a sort of secret."

The thought that he alone knew what was about to happen almost caused him to choke with excitement over his ham and tomatoes. With a broad grin of anticipation he flashed a glance at the top table where the unsuspecting Mr. Wilkins would be sitting. . . . And then the grin faded and his eyes opened wide in shocked surprise. . . . *Mr. Wilkins wasn't there!* Still worse, Mr. Wilkins wasn't anywhere in the room at all!

This was a disaster! This was the end of the carefully planned plot! What on earth would old Jen do when, in a matter of seconds, he made his spectacular entrance? It was too late now to warn him. It was too late, in fact, to do anything but watch in embarrassed silence as Jennings faced his dilemma. . . . Slowly it dawned upon Darbishire that he did *not*, after all, know what was going to happen next!

156

It was at this moment that Mr. Carter rang the bell and called for silence.

"You'll be interested to hear that a most welcome visitor has promised to come along and join us this evening," he announced with a smile. "Indeed, judging from the sleigh parked in the bicycle shed and the team of reindeer grazing on the football pitch, I think that our guest has already arrived and is waiting to come in." He coughed loudly as a signal to his colleague standing in the kitchen with his ear pressed to the crack of the dining hall door.

Mr. Wilkins was prompt on his cue. He knocked on the door seven times in a distinct and rhythmic tattoo.

All heads turned towards the sound, and thus it was that only a few of the boys were aware of a curious sort of echo of the seven taps which came from the door at the opposite end of the room. But Darbishire heard them, and knew only too well what they meant.

Then the door from the kitchen swung open to reveal a tall, burly, red-robed Father Christmas standing on the threshold.

There was a gasp of surprise and delight; and while the shock wave was still running round the room there followed an even greater surprise, which set the onlookers goggling in amazement. . . . For at the same moment that Mr. Wilkins was making his entrance from the kitchen, the door at the far end of the dining-hall was flung wide, and in marched a small-scale parody of the tall figure, swathed from head to foot in red blanket and with festoons of cotton-wool precariously gummed about its face.

The two Father Christmases came to a dead stop and stood staring at each other in astonishment, while the rest of the school swivelled their gaze from end to end of the room like spectators at a tennis match.

"Wow! What's going on," squawked Blotwell. "*Two* Santa Claus'es-es."

"Well, why not?" shrilled Binns. "I expect they're meant to be Big Claus and Little Claus, or even perhaps Father Christmas and Grandfather Christmas."

Curious to know what was afoot, Mr. Wilkins began

to walk down the room. . . . So did Jennings.

Slowly, master and boy advanced past the now silent tables until they met in the middle of the room by the Christmas tree. One glance at the wide-awake eyes peering up at him through the fleecy foliage enabled Mr. Wilkins to identify the uninvited guest.

"Well, well! This is certainly a change in the advertised programme," he said pleasantly. "I never expected to meet a miniature rival engaged on the same errand as myself."

"No, sir, neither did I, sir," came in muffled tones through the barrage of cotton-wool.

"May one inquire the reason for this astounding coincidence?"

"Well, sir, I'm not really supposed to be here at all because of—er—of what you said, sir," Jennings explained. "But I just looked in for a moment to wish you the comps of the season and to give you a present, sir." Whereupon the smaller Father Christmas fumbled in the folds of his blanket and produced a fountain pen which he solemnly handed to his towering colleague.

The taller Father Christmas stared in surprise. Then he accepted the gift with a smile of gratitude. "My fountain pen! How splendid!" he beamed. "That's extremely kind of you, Jennings—er—Santa Claus minor, I should say. And very clever of you to have found it."

"That's all right, sir," said Santa Claus minor.

"Now let me see if I can return the compliment," Mr. Wilkins went on. From a pocket beneath his robe he extracted a battered penknife which he presented to his junior partner. "There you are, Jennings. I shall be honoured if you will accept this—er—this little gift with my best wishes for a happy Christmas."

"Oh, thank you, sir—I mean Father Christmas, sir," Jennings said as he pocketed his precious possession. "You couldn't have given me a better present, honestly, sir."

At that, a thunderous burst of applause rang out from the feasters in the dining-hall. This mutual exchange of gifts was, they felt, well in keeping with the spirit of the occasion. Besides, what better gift could anyone wish for than to have his own lost or confiscated property restored in such a seasonable manner.

"A very fair exchange between one Father Christmas and another," commented Mr. Carter when the cheering had died down.

Jennings shuffled his feet awkwardly. There was still one important matter which had not been mentioned. Now was the time, he decided, to drop a fairly obvious hint.

"I suppose I really ought to be going now, sir," he said diffidently. "I only just—sort of—looked in to give you your pen. You see, I found it in the stationery cupboard, and you said I'd got to stay and tidy it up instead of coming to the party, sir."

The taller Father Christmas was quick to take the hint. "Tut, tut. That was very careless of me," he said, smiling through his beard. "However, after this unexpected display of goodwill I can't very well ask my junior colleague to withdraw, so you'd better stay on and join in the fun."

"Oh, thank you, Father—I mean, thank you, sir—er —Father Christmas, sir," Jennings stammered in delighted confusion. He was about to hurry away to his table when Mr. Wilkins laid a restraining hand on his shoulder.

"Just a minute, Jennings—or Santa Claus minor or Father Christmas Junior, or whatever you're supposed to be."

"Yes, sir?"

"We Father Christmases have a duty to perform," Mr. Wilkins said, waving a hand at the closely-packed tables round the room. "A message of seasonal goodwill to all these people who have come here to enjoy themselves. Let's deliver our greetings together, shall we?"

"Yes, rather, sir."

The two Father Christmases faced their audience and raised their voices in duet. "A very merry Christmas to you all! "

In deafening response, the school echoed the greetings with full-throated cheers that set the windows rattling. As the dust settled, Darbishire's shrill voice could be

159

heard above the tumult reciting a selection of his home-made yuletide poetry.

"And the same to you with lots of good cheer,
From yours truly, C. E. J. Darbi-*SHIRE*."

This provoked a round of applause for the poet who, scarlet in the face with self-conscious pride, took a hasty drink of lemonade to cover his embarrassment. In his flurry he gulped down more than he intended and had to be slapped on the back by his neighbours.

When at last order was restored, the smaller Father Christmas sat down in his place, hurriedly removing those parts of his fast-moulting whiskers which might interfere with the serious business of eating.

He'd have to work fast, he told himself: the rest of the chaps had got to the jelly-and-custard stage already, and here he was with a whole plateful of ham and tomatoes to finish before he caught them up. . . . And after the jelly and custard there would be cakes and mince pies, and after that there would be carol singing, and after that a film show, and after that . . . Well, after that they would go to bed and wake up to find that the holidays had actually started.

Jennings munched on in silence, listening with half an ear to the snippets of conversation going on around him . . . . Binns and Blotwell were arguing happily about the decorations in Form 1 classroom. Venables was pointing out to Atkinson what a kind face Mr. Wilkins seemed to have, now that four-fifths of his features were hidden behind his whiskers. Darbishire was reciting his latest home-made poem to Temple, who was so busy eating that he hadn't got time to listen. Everyone was making a great deal of noise, and everyone was enjoying himself.

This was the place to be, Jennings said to himself: *this* was better than tidying the stationery cupboard! Of course, his little scheme hadn't worked out *quite* as he had expected. . . . Still, it had been worth it. There was nothing like a good dose of festive spirit to round off the Christmas term.

GOOD WORK